A Contemporary "Retro" Romance

Loving Jordan

By

Elizabeth Castle

Name: Castle, Elizabeth, author
Title: Loving Jordan
Description: Series: Contemporary "Retro" Romance Series
Publisher: In The Air Publishing

Identifiers: ISBN 9781967731329 (ebook) | ISBN 9781967731336 (paperback) | ISBN 9798305660166 (amazon hardcover)

Cover Design by betibup33

Chapter One

"I'll be right back with that coffee." Samantha Brody yawned behind a stack of menus. She'd been on her feet since the morning shift, and her body was showing every sign of collapsing. It was almost midnight now. Things were finally starting to slow down. The Saturday night crowd was finally making its way back home. Or to the bar down the street.

Samantha looked over at the clock again. When she had started working here, the restaurant had closed at eleven. By this time on the weekends, she'd have been in her car on her way home, or if she were lucky, already tucked into bed. Now there were almost weekly changes to the restaurant, and the first thing that had changed was the hours. The restaurant opened at five in the morning instead of six. The restaurant closed at two in the morning on Fridays and Saturdays. Thankfully she would be one of the first to leave. Getting home at three in the morning was not on today's to-do list. She was too tired.

Despite the worn-looking booths and threadbare carpet the restaurant sported, business was lively tonight, as it was every weekend. The various diners that evening had been a rowdy crowd and Samantha was worn out from running around. Lanky teenagers who had enough money to waste on things other than fast food had come and gone earlier in the evening, leaving behind a bigger mess than a group of two-year old's. The adults had settled in shortly afterward, their complaints many and varied. There wasn't much to do on a Saturday night in the old mountain town, or any other night for that matter. They came here to Larry's. The food was as uninspired as the restaurant's name. Larry had been the previous owner, more than ten years ago now, but the name had stayed the same.

Samantha glanced out the window to see yet another round of snowfall. The on-again-off-again snow showers looked like they were very much on again. The meteorologists were forecasting snow for the rest of the week. Just the thought of having to leave the warm restaurant was daunting. With the restaurant booths still half full, it was apparent the snow wasn't keeping people indoors.

Knowing the snow was coming, Samantha would have stayed home from work, but such luxuries weren't allowed in her home. Just because she had the worst cold she could ever remember having was no excuse for her to miss work. Her aunt had shooed her out the door that morning, telling her she'd better get her fanny to work. If her aunt could work through a cold in the dead of winter, so could her niece. Samantha would have argued that being a waitress was a lot more difficult than answering phones, but she knew from experience that begging and pleading wouldn't work. It hadn't worked as a child. At twenty-two, it still didn't.

Samantha thought longingly of her bed with its thick handmade quilted blanket. The old quilt her grandmother made was double layered. Grandma Jane had always doubled up her blankets when she decided to make one. She'd lived in Colorado long enough to know that you kept yourself warm in the winter. Unfortunately for Samantha, it would be at least another hour before she could even hope for the luxury of snuggling under her covers. And with the way this crowd was lingering, most likely it would be much longer.

"Yo, Samantha, you awake over there? There's another table to be taken care of. Get going." Roger's chubby face appeared around the corner of the kitchen door.

Samantha glanced around and saw a new group of diners sitting down. Never mind that she was supposed to have left at twelve. When Roger was in charge, he milked every minute out of the staff that he could. Roger's father owned the restaurant, but with the way Roger strutted around the place, you'd think he did. With Roger Senior not bothering to come in these days, it hardly mattered who really owned it. Roger Junior had made various changes to the restaurant, and his father had let him.

Instead of arguing that it was time for her to go, she headed over to the table in the corner that had just been occupied. When she saw who the diners were, she realized there was no way she was getting out of the restaurant any time soon. Amelia Forrester and her current paramour were sitting there, their voices audible over the considerable noise in the restaurant. Usually, Amelia didn't bother eating locally, but when she did, she was sure to make a production of it. She probably had on her most expensive sweater, and the jeans she wore were definitely designer. The boots, too, were designer and made to look good, not to keep her feet warm.   Along with her makeup and hair, she looked extremely out of place in the run-down restaurant.

The Forresters were the wealthiest people in town, probably the wealthiest for miles. The Forresters bred horses, or so they liked to claim. None of them actually had anything to do with the ranch their home was set on. They had people who took care of the ranch for them. They came and went as they pleased. The Forresters had more than one house, although the actual number had yet to be determined. To her knowledge, there was the ranch house, the beach house in Florida, another in the hills of California, and another house in Aspen for the winter ski season. It seemed that the family was back for a while, although Samantha doubted they would be here long. While the children were growing up, the family had lived in Ford Hollow, using their ranch as their home during the school year.

Like most people in town, she didn't see much of the rest of the family, although she knew who they were. The only one she'd met personally was Amelia, and that didn't say much for the rest of the Forrester clan. Amelia was a spoiled brat, not to mention the baby of the family. It showed in every word and every action. Amelia was somebody, or so she thought, and she let everyone know it.

Amelia had just turned twenty-one that year. She'd made a big deal out of it. Samantha was slightly older, but they'd shared a few classes through school. Samantha had missed so much school her freshman year that she'd failed most of her classes. When she'd retaken the ones she'd failed, she had to take them her sophomore year, along with the new batch of freshman. It still grated on her nerves that she'd had to stay home to take care of her aunt, even after all these years. Her aunt had been going through her very first pregnancy that year. She'd eventually lost the child, for which Samantha had felt bad. Her aunt had desperately wanted a child. Vivian had come along soon after, but the loss of her first pregnancy was still something Rose hadn't completely gotten over.

That year had been bad for the small Brody family. Her father had started disappearing more and more, driving his truck for longer stretches at a time. Samantha spent the summer working. When she'd gone back to school, Amelia and her friends had tormented her in the way some high school girls do. Samantha hadn't bothered to take it personally. Amelia tormented everyone. It had just been grating to have her failures tossed in her face by the most popular girl in school day after day.

Samantha shrugged out of her reverie and headed over to take care of the table. High school seemed so long ago and so unimportant in the overall scheme of things.

As Samantha took their order, she didn't know if she should be insulted that Amelia didn't recognize her or not. In all the times she'd dined here, she had never let on that she knew who Samantha was. Unfortunately, it wasn't a sign that Amelia had grown up and had given up her old ways. It just meant that she hadn't cared who she'd tormented enough to remember their names and faces.

Amongst the giggling and fluttering eyelashes, Samantha managed to get their order. She headed back to the kitchen, her legs feeling like lead weights and her head pounding again.

"Figures she'd show up tonight. It's been a long time since she's been around." Katherine Lawson, who insisted that everyone call her Kitty, was a fellow waitress. Her overdone makeup and spiky blond hair peeked through the doors to spy on Amelia. The outrageous hair and makeup amused Samantha, especially since the woman was on the verge of turning fifty. But the older woman had a tall, curvy figure that Samantha envied. Samantha barely topped five feet. Her license said five-two, but it was mostly wishful thinking on Samantha's part. Kitty was five-ten and all leg.

Samantha just shook her head. And immediately regretted it. Her fever must be higher than she thought. Just a little jostle made her dizzy. She focused on the back of Kitty's head, trying to stop the spinning. "It's never long enough. You'd think she'd find someplace else to go and stay there. It's not like this town can offer the fun and excitement she gets elsewhere."

Kitty heard the yawn that interrupted Samantha's words. "You should be getting home. You look dead on your feet."

"I feel dead on my feet. But you know Roger, no one leaves until everything's cleaned up."

Kitty knew Roger well. "That fool hangs around here too much. You'd think a man his age would have something better to do than harass waitresses." Roger had just turned thirty, and he'd had a huge party at the restaurant to celebrate it. He'd made the staff clean up afterward.

Samantha agreed. "The cooks, too. I heard that Becky dumped him. My guess is he'll be around a lot more until he finds a new girlfriend. And let's face it, there aren't that many women to choose from around here who don't already know him, or who haven't already dated him and discovered what a jerk he is."

Becky had been a blessing to the staff. With Roger occupied with his new lady, he spent less time managing the restaurant. His father was a lot more laid-back and didn't treat his staff poorly. When the man fully retired, Samantha was seriously considering trying to find a different job. But in a town this size, there weren't many choices.

Kitty patted Samantha's shoulders, then rubbed them lightly. Samantha knew Kitty was concerned about her. She could hardly blame her. The cough she'd developed was getting worse. She had been sporting fever flags every day this past week. Her already thin frame seemed to be getting even thinner. Her skin lacked all luster, and her eyes were glazed over. But Samantha needed the money. Kitty had commented more than once that this situation was ridiculous, and that no one in their right mind would be working in Samantha's condition. Kitty had gone on to tell her that if she were Samantha's mother, she'd have tied her to the bed to keep her at home. Samantha couldn't argue, because as the minutes ticked by, she felt worse.

Samantha closed her eyes again and propped herself against the counter. She didn't dare sit down. If she did, she might not get back up again. Her already unsteady legs were threatening to dump her on the floor.

Kitty finished up Amelia's table before Samantha could muster the energy to take care of it herself. Samantha couldn't even drum up the energy to argue. When Kitty came back, Samantha barely felt her nudging her awake.

"Samantha, wake up, honey."

Samantha jolted. Dear heaven, she had almost fallen asleep standing up. "I'm up."

Looking for something to keep her awake, Kitty fetched her a cup of coffee. With the way Samantha was feeling, the caffeine wouldn't keep her awake later. And the hot fluid might help with the congestion. "Want to hear the latest gossip?"

She didn't, but Samantha didn't say so. She accepted the coffee gratefully. Despite the heat of the restaurant kitchen, she was shivering. "Sure."

Kitty paused, working up the suspense. "Guess who's back in town?"

Samantha didn't care. "Who?"

Kitty paused again. Then in a whisper, she said, "Jordan Forrester."

That got Samantha's attention. "Are you sure?"

"Yep. Saw him myself at the grocery store just this morning. I tell you, you can't miss Jordan when you see him. If I weren't married and were twenty years younger, I'd be all over that man. He's over six feet and solid muscle. He has this gorgeous blond hair, almost like gold. Makes me jealous every time. It's just not fair that men have hair like that. Anyway, I just happened to run out of milk, and you know how testy Christopher gets when he doesn't have milk for his coffee."

Since Samantha knew Kitty's husband well, she nodded at that. "Go on." Jordan Forrester was big news. His visits created loads of gossip, especially since he came and went quickly and infrequently, usually without being seen. Most people didn't know him very well, and Samantha would bet that most stories about him had been made up to amuse the community. He'd attended military school, so he had rarely been around, even as a child. He'd joined the Navy right out of high school. No one was sure what he was up to these days, but everyone had a theory.

"I don't know much. But he's not staying in the family home. He's been staying in a cabin off the main county road that he had built. My guess is he's here to visit his grandfather. The old man took ill a few months back. Jordan doesn't care much about visiting the rest of his family enough to seek them out more than a couple of times a year. But he and his granddaddy have always been close."

The Forrester's eldest child had left at the age of eighteen. If Samantha got her math right, that would make him thirty-one now. He came back now and again, usually around the holidays, but no one seemed to know what he'd been up to. As the oldest of three children, and the only male, his activities had been closely monitored as he'd grown up. When he'd decided to forgo joining the family business and had sought his fortunes elsewhere, the town had been shocked. No one turned their back on the Forrester family, especially one of its own. But the family business was being run by the husband of the oldest sister, Lillian, and Jordan was usually nowhere to be found.

"I doubt he's here to stay, even if he did have a cabin built." Samantha had never met Jordan Forrester and didn't know what he looked like. She had only ever seen his sister and mother, who had hair darker than her own auburn shade and brown eyes instead of blue. Kitty said he had blond hair, but it was hard to picture it. But it didn't matter that she'd never set eyes on Jordan before. She had lived in this small community all her life, and any news about the Forresters spread like wildfire, and she listened as intensely as everyone else.

The whole family was of interest, although Samantha didn't always pay close attention to the gossip. The rest of the family wasn't nearly as interesting to hear about. Jordan's father had been mayor once. Then he'd been a state representative. He'd given up politics in the last few years when he'd lost a race for senator. It had pleased most everyone in town to not have his influence over them anymore, but he still had big money, and that money still held power.

Jordan's mother had been born in New Hampshire. When or how the elder Forrester had met his bride, no one was sure. He'd just come back from a visit back east one day with a wife in tow. Three children followed: Jordan, Lillian, and Amelia.

Samantha gave a little more thought to Jordan and his family before she pushed them from her mind and got back to work. She'd met one of the Forresters, and one was enough. And that one was currently demanding her attention. After Amelia exclaimed disgustedly that she'd tasted better sewage, she and her date left the restaurant. Samantha was not surprised to see no tip left on the table. Amelia never left one. She found some reason to hate the food or the service right before she had to pay the check.

Kitty helped clean up the restaurant, noticing the lack of tip. Samantha watched Kitty from the corner of her eye, knowing she'd try to slip some extra money on the table. Over the last few years of working together, Samantha had caught her more than once. Kitty had gotten pretty good at slipping a few dollars into Samantha's tips. Her concern warmed her, so she did her best to slip the money back to her without her noticing.

"Are you going to be all right, hon?" Kitty was watching her as she swayed on her feet. Samantha knew she needed to be in bed. And with the way she was going, she was soon going to need a hospital bed if she didn't get some rest.

"I'm fine." The coughing fit that followed that statement made Kitty skeptical.

Samantha knew Kitty didn't believe a word she said and was touched when Kitty followed behind her all the way home. Samantha drove home slowly with Kitty trailing behind her until she pulled into her aunt's driveway and got through the front door. Since it was on Kitty's way home anyway, Samantha didn't fuss. Samantha waved at her friend, letting her know she knew exactly what Kitty had been up to. It warmed her. Kitty had a big, generous heart.

The house was dark when Samantha unlocked the front door, as it always was when she worked the evening shift. Her aunt would have been in bed hours ago. She kept early nights. She claimed that she needed her beauty sleep. If any woman needed it, it was her aunt. By the end of the day, her aunt looked drawn and tired. She'd fix dinner, watch her favorite nighttime shows, and go off to bed. Despite the somewhat boring existence, her aunt was happy with her routine and became agitated when it was disrupted.

Samantha climbed the two small steps that led to the

addition in the back. The house had been built with only two small bedrooms, a kitchen, a living room, and a tiny bath. The previous owner had added a large room in the back of the house. It was drafty and not that well built, but it gave Samantha the privacy she craved. Her aunt had one bedroom, and her sister Vivian had the other. Since her sister was only five, she had taken over most of the house with her toys. A few even dotted her own bedroom floor. Her aunt doted on her only daughter and let her have the run of the house.

Samantha stifled another coughing fit and stripped out of her uniform. She hung it up neatly because she'd need it again in the morning and just didn't have the energy to run it through the wash. She had to be back at work by ten, and if she wanted to get any sleep, washing the uniform would have to wait. Monday she didn't have to be in until the dinner shift, and she'd have the opportunity to catch up on her sleep, along with the laundry and a multitude of other chores.

Samantha tossed on a robe and headed for the bathroom. Looking in the mirror was a mistake. She looked terrible. The dark auburn hair that she'd tied back earlier was hanging limply around her face now that she'd released it from its tight bun. Her usually rosy skin was white. Her usually lively dark blue eyes were flat, tired. In the last two weeks since she'd gotten sick, the weight she'd lost was apparent in her face. Her cheeks were sunken in and her lips were pale and dry. It was no wonder Kitty had been so concerned.

She quickly showered and dried her hair. She wasn't

hungry, so she didn't bother to go find what her aunt had fixed for dinner. She wouldn't be able to choke down a single bite. Her stomach was roiling again from the two cups of coffee at work, and she felt like she'd be sick at any moment. She shrugged into her warmest nightshirt and went to bed.

But dawn came too soon. Vivian was awake, and she was not a quiet child. Samantha rolled over to glance at the clock. It was only seven. She'd only been in bed for a little over four hours. It might as well not have been any for the way she felt. Her throat hurt worse than it did the day before; her head was pounding in tandem with her sister's playful giggling. Her body ached everywhere, and she was shivering under her covers.

Samantha barely had time to brace herself when her sister slung open the bedroom door and jumped on her. The low moan of pain went unheeded as Vivian began bouncing up and down, demanding a bowl of cereal. A voice from the hall called Vivian out of her bed. Samantha groaned as the voices continued. Vivian was being lectured about waking people up, a lecture that was given almost every morning.

"I'm up." Samantha struggled out of her covers but moaned again when the cold air hit her bare legs.

"Come on and get some breakfast then." Rose Brody shook her head at her daughter and left Samantha where she was.

Samantha let her head hang for a moment, then pushed the tangles back. She and her aunt didn't always get along well. Rose had taken care of Samantha for most of her teenage years. Samantha's dad had married his deceased wife's sister, and Rose made sure Samantha was fed and clothed. She just had never been an affectionate woman. The years after Vivian had been born was a revelation. Rose was a doting, loving mother to Vivian. Even now that her husband had left, she still retained an open affection for her only daughter.

Some things never changed, and Samantha had given up trying to change them. Her father was gone for good and had been for three years. Samantha was content with the relationship she had with her aunt. They were roommates and somewhat friends. It was more than she'd had growing up.

She made it through breakfast, thankfully not a bowl of cold cereal, and managed polite conversation. Her aunt must have noticed how sick she was because she fixed another hot cup of coffee for her. The medicine she'd taken helped her breathe a little better and stopped the nagging cough. But by the time she was dressed and ready for work, she was dragging.

The bathroom mirror showed her she was in pretty bad shape and that the little sleep she'd gotten had not helped. The hair that was washed the night before was matted to her head. With the help of a few pins and a thick brush, she managed to get it into its regular twist. She would love to leave it down, but the restaurant frowned on leaving hair loose, even in a ponytail. She decided to forego makeup today. Her skin was so pale that anything more than a little blush was going to make her look ridiculous. She tried a little concealer and mascara, but it didn't look good, and she took it off. There was nothing she could do about it, so she powdered her face and left the bathroom.

Her uniform needed washing, but that would come tonight. It was still mostly clean but a little wrinkled. Samantha managed to get into her pantyhose, socks, and shoes. She grabbed a sweater and tossed it over the uniform. Roger hated his employees wearing anything but the uniform. It was simply too bad, she told herself; she was freezing. She grabbed her purse, checking its contents.

It had taken a bit longer than usual to get ready for work, but Samantha didn't rush. Her body wouldn't have let her. She simply bid her aunt and sister goodbye, not having the energy to play with Vivian as she usually did. It had snowed through the night, and it made getting to work that much more difficult. She'd managed to warm up the car and clear off the snow, but it was slow going. Roger used any reason he could to dock his workers' pay, and being late was his favorite. Thankfully, she managed to get there on time.

The late morning shift drifted into dinner. Sundays were always busy. The church crowd was good for tips, but today Samantha would have given anything to still be curled up in bed. She'd not gotten enough sleep and her head was woozy. Her body felt like it was on autopilot. She managed to screw up several orders, but no one complained too loudly. She had a feeling that her illness showed, and her customers felt sorry for her.

As was usual, she stayed past the time she was scheduled. The restaurant could use another waitress, but Samantha doubted Roger would hire anyone else. Since she usually picked up the extra, it would only cut into her own hours.

She stayed through lunch, stayed through the early afternoon, and somehow made it through the early dinner crowd.

It wasn't that late when she left, but it was dark and had been for a few hours. The snow was blowing sideways across the parking lot as Samantha let herself out. She wrapped her coat tighter around herself, fruitlessly trying to keep the draft from going up her back. It took her already frozen fingers a moment to unlock her car door. Thankfully the door wasn't frozen shut. It was colder this winter than it had been in a long time. It didn't look like the cold was going to let up.

When Samantha managed to get into her car, it sputtered and choked a bit in the cold. Nervously she tried the key again. When the car finally started up, she gave a quick thanks, flicking on the defrost. She would have hated to have to call her aunt to come get her. It would have been such a hassle to get Vivian dressed for the cold. Plus, she couldn't afford to fix the car if it were having serious trouble. Despite her hope that the car only needed to warm up, the car kept rattling as she made her way home. Because of the snow, she was driving much slower than she wished.

Halfway home, it seemed the wind was howling louder. Then she realized the sound was coming from the car. A weird hissing noise assailed her ears. The sound just kept getting louder, and not knowing what to do, Samantha pulled over to the shoulder. The noise was getting louder even as the car idled. She shut the engine off for a moment to listen. She looked around. She was a mile or so from home. The familiar road up ahead had her trying the key again. Hopefully her car would make it the rest of the way.

But when she tried the key, the engine wouldn't start. "Please don't do this now." Samantha's head was pounding, and her throat was aching again. The car was getting colder by the second. Her breath was starting to be visible again in the confines of the car. She kept trying the key, but after a minute, Samantha realized the car wasn't going to start.

Tears of frustration filled her eyes. This couldn't be happening. She was too tired and too sick to deal with the cold and blowing snow. Though she was on a main road, it could be a long time before anyone came by. And it wasn't a guarantee that they'd stop and check on the broken-down car. She couldn't fix it herself; she could change the oil and check her fluids, but that was the extent of her knowledge.

She knew that when stranded in a snowstorm, you should wait in your car until someone came along. But this wasn't exactly a well populated area. Samantha looked out the front windshield again. The wind wasn't blowing as hard as it had been when she left the restaurant. Either that or the trees that lined the street kept it from whipping across the road. It wouldn't take long to walk the rest of the way, would it? Samantha pulled her coat tighter around her neck, shivering in her seat. Her coat was warm enough, but her legs would freeze if she tried to walk. Her uniform was a calf-length skirt, and her nylons didn't offer any protection from the cold.

Either way, she couldn't sit here forever. Samantha kept a blanket in the trunk of the car so she could wrap it around her waist. Hopefully it would keep her legs from freezing. She had on thick shoes and socks so she would be able to walk through the drifts.

Unfortunately, it was easier said than done. As Samantha made it to the trunk, the wind decided to pick up. Mercifully, the blanket was in the trunk, along with her boots. She smiled briefly. She'd forgotten that she'd put them there. An extra red scarf and her ski gloves were there, too. She must be truly exhausted to have forgotten. She'd spent enough years in the cold winter to be prepared, just in case. If only she'd thought to put a pair of pants in there. But she made do with the blanket.

Trying not to open her coat too much, she hiked up the knee-length coat to her waist. She managed to get the blanket around her, despite the blowing wind. She tied it tightly around her hips and managed to slip on the boots by leaning up against the car. She tied the scarf around her head to keep her ears warm and pulled her hood up over it. The rest of the scarf was long enough to get across her face if she held it. She wouldn't freeze on the way home. She slammed the trunk shut and tucked her small purse into the pocket of her coat.

Samantha started on her way, keeping her head bent low. But between the wind and her fatigue, the going was slow. The snow was falling harder now, and it was getting hard to see. She turned back to see how far she'd gone and realized she hadn't gone very far. Her car could still be seen despite poor visibility. How was she going to make it home? She had only gone a few yards, and already her legs were aching and cold. It would take forever to get home. If only there were a house nearby. But the only thing close was the small stretch of homes where she lived.

Samantha stopped for a moment. Her chest hurt, and it felt like her lungs were freezing. Every breath was painful. Despite the boots and thick socks, her feet were frozen. Her legs were going numb. The cold was making her eyes water. She kept trudging on, watching her feet.

She had no idea how far she'd gone. She tried to turn around, but her body wouldn't cooperate. Samantha's head spun, and the ground seemed to be getting closer. She never knew she had passed out.

Chapter Two

Jordan Forrester lounged by the fire, listening to his father drone on. He stifled a yawn and kept a look of boredom on his face. If he hadn't already had to listen to this lecture, he might have tolerated it a bit better. But he was tired. He'd spent the last three days being lectured on and off during his visits, and he didn't know how much more he could take. Jordan had spent so much time arguing that he was simply worn out. Why, he wondered, had it been less tiring as a child to argue with his father? Was it simply age? If that were so, then his father should be on the verge of collapse. But he was just hitting his lecturing stride, oblivious to the fact that his son was not listening anymore.

Jordan's gaze wandered from the hypnotic fire to his grandfather. The old man had the nerve to wink at him. His grandfather had been sitting quite contentedly, listening to his only son lecture his only grandson. He knew how hard Jordan had fought for his independence through the years, yet the older man said nothing to interrupt.

"Dad, when are you going to simply accept that I don't want to work for you? You have Lillian working for you. And her husband. He runs the company better than I ever could."

Philip ignored him. "It's time you stopped playing around. There are several branches you could work for.

You could find something that interests you. We own enough small businesses that you could find one that you could take over. Wet your feet. You don't have to take over the entire corporation yet."

Jordan set down his glass of brandy. He hadn't wanted it in the first place, but his father had poured it and ignored his protests. He always ignored his protests when he was in this mood. "I told you I like what I do."

Philip kept on. "You do nothing. You take pictures. That's not a job; it's a hobby. You can't support a family with your camera."

"My family can support itself." Jordan knew which direction the conversation was going, and he tried to derail it.

"You know I mean a wife and children of your own. You're thirty-one. You should be married already. By the time I was your age, I had a wife and two children."

"I know that. You tell me every time I see you. And I keep telling you I'm not interested in a wife and kids. Despite what you think, if I had them, I could support them just fine with my photographs."

"I don't see how. The least you could have done was stay in the Navy. You would at least have a steady income instead of the trickles you get from your pictures."

"Let the boy be, Philip. You've harassed him enough for today." Lionel Forrester had heard enough. His grandson looked ready to leave. With the snow falling as heavily as it was, the boy shouldn't be out driving around.

"I wouldn't have to if he'd listen." Philip sank into the chair near his son, letting the fire warm his hands. He dropped silent, the lecture over for now.

Jordan gave silent thanks. He hated coming home and listening to how he'd failed the family. He hadn't wanted to get into law and politics like his father. He hadn't wanted to get into business like his grandfather. Only his grandfather seemed to understand his need to find his own way. And the pictures he took, despite the fact that he hated hearing his work being described in such lowbrow terms, were doing well for him. And if they didn't, he had enough job experience from his time in the Navy and after the Navy to get a decently paying job. He could even go back to school if he wanted.

As far as a wife and family went, he still had time. He'd never admit it to his father, but he knew he would have a family eventually. He'd not met the right woman, and he wasn't one to settle. He liked the idea of having a family. Despite his disagreements with his father, he loved him and knew his father returned the sentiment. They were just too stubborn to get along. His mother gave up years ago trying to influence him. Now she just enjoyed his visits. If only he could get his father to be the same way, he could extend his visits.

Jordan glanced down discreetly at his fancy gold watch, a birthday gift from his mother. It was almost eight. He looked out the window to see the snow blowing and to hear the wind howling. He should have left hours ago. He was enjoying the solitude of his cabin and was anxious to get back. He'd had it built for the purpose of relaxation, and a place to escape from his family when he needed to when he visited. The construction had just been finished last month, and it had been the best idea he'd had in years. This vacation was something he needed. He'd only been here four days, and he'd already had the chance to catch up on some of his reading and enjoy sitting around doing nothing.

"Not thinking of driving out in that, are you?" Lionel saw his grandson checking his watch and the window.

"I have to. I need to get back to McKinley." Jordan had brought the cat with him to have just that very excuse. He could have let a friend take care of him for a few weeks, but he'd brought the cat with. He wasn't very big, so he was easy to pack up. And for some reason, the cat seemed to enjoy the car.

Philip glanced up from the fire. "The cat will be fine. You're not driving out in this snow."

Jordan sighed. He really was getting tired of arguing. "Sorry. It won't be too bad right now. I might be snowed in by morning, though." Please, he thought. A nice blizzard to trap him in his cabin would be wonderful.

He rose. The easiest thing to do was simply ignore them and leave. But things were never easy. His mother met him in the hall, her eyes filled with worry. "It's snowing much too hard out there for you to go back to your cabin." She refused to say "home."

He kissed his mother's cheek and gave her hand a quick squeeze, all the while circling around her to the door. "I'll call as soon as I get home. Besides, I have four-wheel drive. I'll be fine."

Ellen knew when her son was determined. "All right. But you had better call. I know you have a cell phone, so you can't use the excuse that the phone lines were down to avoid calling me."

Jordan nodded. He didn't have a phone at the cabin, but he didn't tell her that. She would demand that he get one once she realized she couldn't always get through to him on his cell due to the interference of the mountains. For now, she was content with his cell number. He closed the door behind him when he heard his father calling his name. He hurried to his truck, knowing that he'd be facing another argument if he didn't hurry. He was halfway down the driveway before his father made it to the front door.

As he made his way down the country roads, he began to seriously reconsider what he was doing. The snow was piling up rapidly. There was already a foot of snow on the ground, although it had taken more than two days to pile up. It seemed as if another foot had fallen since he'd headed out that morning. The roads were plowed but not well. Visibility was worsening, especially now since it was pitch-black outside.

He probably should have stayed put. He just hadn't been able to handle his father anymore. His mother said they were a lot alike. Jordan agreed. They both were cut from the same cloth, despite the differences in opinion about his career.

The only thing Jordan had inherited from his father was his blond hair. The color had served Philip well over the years while he was in politics. They had called him the "golden boy" of politics. Never mind that his father had been in his forties at the time. He had his grandfather's amber-colored eyes instead of his father's blue ones. Despite the hair, he didn't look much like his father. His father was a good-looking man. Jordan had the more carved features of his grandfather. His face didn't have any softness in it like his father's more rounded features. He had his grandfather's high brows and blade of a nose. He had a square chin and deep-set cheekbones. Only his lips relieved the planes of his face, and they were probably a tad larger than they should be on a face so harshly carved. Handsome was not a word used to describe Jordan. Striking was the word he'd heard used, and he decided it probably fit.

The men also shared the same stubborn personality. Jordan blamed Lionel for it. Despite the different physical appearances of the three men, they were all proud men. They would fight to the death to uphold their principles. The arguments that had taken place between the three men were legendary. Only Lionel had mellowed over the years. Philip was, and would always be, hardheaded. It was the only term Jordan had come up with that suited his father. His father returned the sentiment.

As Jordan made it to the main road without any trouble and the driving improved, he was glad he opted to leave. Family reunions never went well for the first week. He would have a sore jaw in the morning from clenching his teeth. Once the first few days were over, Jordan would be able to relax and enjoy his family.

Jordan glanced at the dash. It was eight thirty. He was only a few minutes from the cabin. He'd had it built close enough to the family home to make the drive a pleasant one. But far enough away that the distance couldn't be walked.

Jordan turned onto the road that took him home. The

cabin was just off the road but hidden by trees. In this weather, he might just miss his driveway. It was only big enough for one vehicle and was easily missed.

But as he slowed his vehicle to make the turn onto the road, he lost control of the truck. He could see a car in front of him a short distance away. He knew not to panic. Despite years of driving in snowy conditions, his truck spun out of control. His truck slammed into the smaller car, pushing it further off the road. He hit his head on the steering wheel and passed out.

* * *

A flurry of white was all Jordan could see. He lifted his hand to press to his head. For some reason, it hurt. He leaned back, keeping his hand pressed to the center of his forehead. The pain was receding, and he couldn't feel anything wet or sticky, which meant no cut.

Knowledge came back when he saw the back window of a car in front of him. He'd lost control of the truck when he hit a patch of ice. Had the car not been parked where it was, none of this would have happened. He would have regained control before going into the ditch.

But first things first. Why was the car parked there? Jordan hoped no one was in the car. The last thing he needed was to have injured someone. He zipped his coat up and grabbed the hat he kept in the glove compartment. He tugged it over his head and stepped out of the truck.

It was getting colder. The snow looked like it was tapering off, but the temperature was plummeting. If the thermometer didn't drop well below zero tonight, he'd be surprised. Jordan looked around but didn't see anything coming or going. The only sound was the crunch of his boots in the snow. He'd worn hiking boots to his parents' house, but he certainly hadn't expected to need them for hiking tonight. But his truck was in a ditch, and with this snow, the chances of getting it back out again without help were slim. Luckily, he'd gone off the road close to his driveway. It wouldn't take long to walk back to the cabin. But first, he needed to see if there was anyone in the car.

Jordan cursed, remembering that he hadn't grabbed a flashlight, but the moon was bright enough at the moment to see in. He couldn't see anyone inside, but to be sure, he yanked the door open. When no scream or angry shout assailed his ears, he let out a sigh of relief. Thank goodness there wasn't anyone inside. He'd worry about the insurance aspect of it later. Right now, he was freezing.

Jordan trudged back to his truck and climbed in. He started the engine to warm himself back up. The time showed he'd only been out for a couple of minutes. He must have just been dazed a bit from the impact, not seriously hurt. But five minutes later he had to accept defeat. The truck wasn't getting out of the ditch tonight. He didn't have much choice. The walk would be a cold one, but he'd be fine. He had a warm coat on, even if it was only hip length. The hat would keep his head warm, which was the best he could do. He checked his pockets for his gloves. He pulled them out and smiled. He wasn't as prepared as he could have been, but he wouldn't freeze. Winters here in the mountains could be cold, but they were nothing compared to the winter he'd spent with his camera in the northernmost parts of Alaska.

Jordan tucked his cell phone in his pocket, knowing there would be hell to pay if he didn't call his mother. He contemplated doing it now, but was afraid she might know he wasn't back home yet. Mothers had ways of knowing those sorts of things. He turned off the engine and stepped out of the truck. Now was the best time to get moving. The snow had let up, but he knew it would be a brief reprieve. The sooner he got going, the sooner he could plop down in front of the fireplace. Most people would be warm and cozy inside, not out driving around in a mini blizzard.

He passed the other car. It wasn't going anywhere either. He hoped whoever had been driving it was having better luck than he was. He hadn't been walking for five minutes when the sight of his driveway was lit by the growing moonlight. He looked at the woods, contemplating cutting through. His driveway wouldn't have been plowed yet, so he was going to have to walk through the snow no matter what.

He started to turn away from the road when the wind kicked up again. Something fluttered and caught his eye. He stopped, tucking his head down until the sudden wind stopped. But the flash of something came again. Cursing a bit under his breath, he headed back to the side of the road where he'd been walking.

Whatever it was, it was red. The closer he got to the object in the snow, the harder his heart started beating. A large shape was covered by a thin layer of snow, and the red item that was flashing looked like a scarf. He realized that his fear was right. It was a person lying in the snow. From the size, he feared it was a child. He ran the rest of the way, managing not to stumble in the deep snow.

The body was lying on its side; its back to him. The scarf had worked itself free from around the head and had blown up over the hood. First aid training came back to him, and he prayed that he wouldn't need it.

Puffs of air were coming from behind a piece of coat that was pulled up over the face. He was afraid that there might be a head injury or something, but he couldn't just leave the body lying on the side of the road. A brief check told him that whoever it was, they weren't seriously injured. Or at least, they didn't have a serious head injury. He gently rolled the body over onto its back, mindful of a potential back injury. He worked down the oversized coat and checked for a pulse. The pulse was strong. He let out a quick thanks.

It, or rather she, was female and definitely not a child. Although he wouldn't doubt that whoever she was, she was young. The moonlight trailed across her face, revealing lips that were steadily turning blue and pale skin. He had no way of knowing how long she had been lying in the snow.

"Can you hear me?" Jordan shouted to be heard over the sudden wind. He looked up and the sky was darkening again. It seemed the reprieve was to be brief. It still felt like it was getting colder. Either that or he was just getting colder and imagining things.

He shouted again but still got no response. "Come on, lady. Wake up. I can't carry you home." Still no answer.

The woman's breathing was audible. Despite the pale

skin and her freezing body, he had a feeling she was running a fever. Her breathing sounded congested and wheezy. He had to get her warm. Fast.

He brushed the snow off the side of her face and tucked the scarf ends and her coat back around her face. He felt something strange wrapped around her legs. He smiled slightly down at the thick blanket. Then he remembered the car. This must have been the driver. But despite the warm layers she'd wrapped around herself, she hadn't made it far. Dear heaven, he hoped when he got her back to the cabin she wasn't hurt. Her lying unconscious in a ditch could just be because she'd fallen. Or it could mean she was hit by a car. She wouldn't be the first person to have been walking on the shoulder of the road and gotten hit.

He wrapped the blanket tighter around her, managed to get his arms under her, and hiked her up. He grunted a bit but didn't lose hold of her. She wasn't heavy, but he was cold, and his body was stiffening. His fingers were frozen despite the gloves. Besides that, trying to walk through the deep snow was hard enough without having the weight of a small woman in his arms. He shifted her until she was lying over his shoulder. He prayed that she hadn't been hit by a car because if she had been, he didn't want to contemplate internal injuries.

He thought of his cell phone in his pocket but decided against it. Right now, he was her best hope. He couldn't leave her in the snow until help came. And with this weather, there were probably accidents all over the place, and this wasn't exactly a large town. Getting help out here wasn't always an easy task.

Jordan shifted her weight again, a bit higher on his shoulder and was rewarded with a moan. At least she wasn't completely unconscious if she moaned, but she wasn't stirring on his shoulder or trying to wiggle down. He turned back into the snowy woods and cut through them. It was quicker this way. He hoped.

The wind picked up again and Jordan cursed. It was blowing loose snow in his face, making it difficult to see, but after a few more minutes of walking with his head down, he saw his cabin. The light he'd left on was off, which meant the electricity was out. No big surprise there, he thought. Snowstorms usually managed to knock them out. He had a generator on order, but it wasn't in yet. He cursed his luck but kept on. By the time he reached the front door of his cabin, his entire body was aching. His legs hurt from carrying the extra weight through snowdrifts and his shoulder was aching fiercely. Jordan was grateful he was in good shape. His time in the Navy had made him very aware of his body, both his strengths and his weaknesses.

The door blew open when he unlatched it, and he, along with his bundle and a big swirl of snow, dropped onto the cabin floor. He managed to kick the door shut behind him. It was cold inside, which meant the heat had been out for some time. He shifted the woman onto her back but left her bundled up. First, he had to get the fire going. Not only would it heat the cabin, but it would allow him to check the woman better. She hadn't made another sound after that moan, but she didn't seem to be in worse shape.

He got the fire going and looked back over at the woman. She made another small noise, but that was it. He looked around the bare cabin and back to the woman. It had been a long time since he'd had to use his first aid training, but living in Alaska taught you all you ever needed to know about the cold. He shrugged off his coat and tossed it where he'd thrown his gloves. The hat followed. He rose and looked over at his bed. He had bought a cheap full-size mattress to tide him over until he went furniture shopping. He decided the best thing to do would be to drag it by the fire. The woman was still breathing, and she was starting to stir.

After he got the mattress off the wood frame and in front of the fire, he went to the woman. He unwrapped the snow-encrusted blanket from around her legs. She had a skirt on and nylons. Since they seemed reasonably dry, he left them on. He saw the thick snow boots and hoped they had kept her toes warm. He hated to think about frostbite, but it was something to worry about. He yanked her boots off and was rewarded with another small sound. Her feet looked all right through the nylons, but he decided not to take any chances. With a brief apology, he lifted up her skirt and managed to get the nylons off. A brief exam told him her feet were cold but not frozen.

He got up for a moment and went to one of his suitcases. He found a thick pair of socks and a pair of flannel pajama bottoms that he kept around in case he spent the night at his parents. They were drawstring and would fit her well enough to stay on. He managed to get her feet into the socks and work the flannel bottoms over her legs.

He glanced up when she tried to roll over, but she began coughing and stayed where she was. He lifted her up against his chest until the coughing stopped. Her eyelashes fluttered open for a moment. He could see the deep blue of her eyes, but they didn't seem to focus. Her eyes closed again.

He shifted her back away from him while talking to her softly. He unwrapped the scarf from around her head and undid the buttons of her coat. He managed to get it off of her. She didn't stir again. She had a sweater on, but it was unbuttoned. It didn't seem to be very warm to him. He was sure he had something better. But for now, he wanted her under the covers and by the fire.

He lifted her up into his arms again and carried her the short distance to the bed. He set her down and noticed the name tag on her dress. It was a uniform from the restaurant in town, if he wasn't mistaken. She must have been on her way home from work.

At least he had a name. He tried waking her again. "Samantha, can you hear me? Come on, wake up."

All he got was her eyes opening briefly. She tried to say something, but nothing came out. Jordan gave up when she fell back unconscious. She seemed unhurt, which relieved him. She had responded to him, and for the moment, that was good enough. He wrapped her up in a thick blanket, leaving her where she was for the moment.

Jordan stripped off his own boots and socks. Since she had his pajamas, he dug out a pair of sweatpants and another pair of socks. He found a sweatshirt and a sweater. Figuring the sweatshirt would be warmer, he tugged his sweater on over his shirt and went back to Samantha. He pulled off her thin sweater and tugged the sweatshirt over her head. She coughed again, but otherwise didn't move.

Since both of them were dry, he climbed under the blankets with her. The fire was heating the cabin quickly, but he was still shivering a bit. And if he was still cold, it was a sure bet she was.

How long had she been in the snow? Her cough didn't sound new. And although a fever from exposure wasn't uncommon, he had to wonder if that was its cause. Looking at her now, she looked more than cold. Her lips were back to a normal color, but they were dry. Her skin was warming from the fire, but she was still pale. The fever flags on her cheeks could be from the cold, but he doubted it.

But it was her heavy cough that made him wonder if she was sick. It would account for her having passed out in the snow. There hadn't been any visible injuries, and although it was cold, she hadn't gotten far from her car. She should have been able to make it much further, with or without the snow and cold.

He heard a jingling noise and groaned. He'd bet it was his mother on the other end of that jingling. He rose from the bed and found his coat. He was much warmer now, so he tucked the covers tighter around Samantha.

He answered the phone as he finished tucking her in. "Hello, Mom."

"Where are you?"

He smiled at her tone and was grateful that she couldn't see him. "I just got home."

"It's been over an hour. You promised to call."

He glanced down at Samantha, happy when she tried to turn over. Tucked as she was, she wasn't going to get far, but the movement reassured him. He heard his mother again, grumbling in his ear about irresponsible behavior. "I'm sorry, but I had a little accident."

Her shout caused Jordan to pull the phone away from his ear. "I knew it. I told you not to leave, but you did anyway. You could have been killed!"

Jordan saw Samantha's eyes open and this time they held his. "I know, Mom. But I'm home and in one piece." He knelt on the side of the bed, helping Samantha sit up since she seemed determined. She broke into a cough before she got all the way up.

"Who is that, Jordan?"

Jordan realized his mother had heard Samantha's cough. This should be a fun explanation. But it would also serve as an explanation to Samantha, who was eyeing him warily. She wasn't in a panic yet, but she looked like she might try to run at any second.

Jordan took a step back and held up a hand. "I hit a parked car on the side of the road and ended up in a ditch. The woman you just heard is the owner of that car. I didn't know what else to do, so I brought her home until I can get a tow truck."

The answer seemed to appease both his mother and Samantha, who now looked like she was remembering what had happened. He watched as Samantha gave up trying to sit up and lay back down.

"Thank heavens you're both all right. The last thing you need is a lawsuit." Ellen gave up berating her son. "Did you call for help?"

Jordan walked over to the fire and tossed on another log.

He watched as Samantha's eyes followed his movements. "I didn't call for help because it seemed easier to bring her here. Neither of us is hurt. When it stops snowing, I can call and get a tow truck, but it would be best to wait until morning."

He talked to his mother for another moment and then bid her goodnight. "She worries," he said, addressing Samantha.

Samantha nodded. It seemed easier than trying to talk. Her throat hurt and her head was pounding. She remembered her car breaking down. She remembered bundling up and heading off to walk home. She must have passed out in the snow. If this man hadn't come along when he did, she might have frozen to death, buried under the snow. Samantha began to cry. She rolled over onto her side, tucking her legs up under her. She was cold; her body hurt, her car was dead on the side of the road, and she could have frozen to death, and no one would have found her.

"Hey, it's all right." Jordan had seen the glisten of tears in her eyes and wanted to stop them before they became full-fledged. "It's been a rough night."

She sniffled a bit at his soft tone and tucked her head closer to her knees. Everything tonight had been a disaster. Her aunt must be getting worried. Samantha jolted at the thought. She wiped her eyes with the back of her hand and addressed the man who'd rescued her for the first time. "Can I use your phone?"

Jordan slipped it out of his pocket and handed it to her. He'd expected the tears to last a lot longer, but she seemed to have pulled herself together without shedding them.

"Here."

Samantha struggled to sit up. The blanket dropped and she realized that she wasn't wearing her clothes. Or not only her clothes. She could see her uniform skirt hanging out from under the heavy sweatshirt she was wearing. And underneath, she could see blue and gray flannel pants. She wiggled her toes and found oversized socks.

She looked up into the man's face. "I can't even begin to thank you."

Jordan shrugged his shoulders at that. "I'm just glad I found you. If I had cut through the woods, I never would have seen you."

Samantha digested that for a moment. She'd come closer to freezing to death than she wanted to contemplate. "I have to call home."

Jordan nodded. She probably had a boyfriend or husband to call. He'd first thought she was a teenager, but she was definitely not a kid. She had a nice, if small, curvy body that could only belong to a grown woman. He guessed she was over twenty, but just barely.

"Hi, Aunt Rose, it's Samantha." She winced as she heard her aunt berate her for waking her up. "I'm not at work. I..."

Jordan heard her aunt interrupt her, and Samantha grew quiet. He couldn't make out what the woman was saying, but it didn't sound happy.

"Aunt Rose, please. My car broke down and I was stranded." She paused. "No, I'm not at the police station. A gentleman found me. No. I'm fine." Another pause. "I won't be back for a while. It's cold and snowing and I can't leave because the car doesn't work. No, his car is in the same ditch."

Samantha's eyes started to close as she listened to her aunt. "No, I don't work until tomorrow night. No, I didn't get to the bank. I'm sorry. I'll talk to you when I know I'm on my way home." Samantha shut off the phone and stared bleary-eyed at the glowing buttons.

Jordan took the phone from her and eased her back down. "You should sleep."

Samantha just looked up at him for a second, then struggled against his hand. "I need my coat."

Jordan's mouth tightened. "You're not leaving."

Samantha frowned. "I know that. But I need my coat."

Jordan frowned back at her but went and fetched her coat. She grabbed the coat and began frantically searching the pockets. "My purse is gone."

Jordan took the coat from her. He searched the pockets himself. "It must have fallen out." Probably when he'd turned her over his shoulder. He didn't remember anything falling, but it could have been jostled out.

Samantha stared up at him. It couldn't be gone. She had her aunt's paycheck in it and all her tips for the week. There had been almost five hundred dollars in that purse. She had been late for work. She was going to drop it into the night deposit box but had forgotten about it on her way home. When her aunt found out, she would be furious. They needed that money to make the mortgage payment.

Samantha stared up at the man in front of her. She didn't know how things could possibly get worse. It seemed that she was destined to live her life struggling, and right now she'd run out of energy to fight. Her eyes filled helplessly. Horrified at the tears dripping down her cheeks, she curled up in a ball and wept.

Chapter Three

Jordan watched as she shut down. Her skin, unbelievably, was paler than before. She was trembling now, and she hadn't been before. Discomfort at her tears caused his words to come out sounding angry. "Everything can be replaced. There's no need to cry about it. When the snow melts a bit, you and I can try to find it."

Samantha knew it was hopeless. If it had fallen on the side of the road, it was long gone. The plows would be coming through, and it would be swept away. She and her aunt were in big trouble. Samantha would be in big trouble. She rolled onto her stomach, still curled up, and closed her eyes. She didn't need a stranger trying to placate her. He had sounded angry when she started crying, not that she could blame him. No one wanted to be cooped up with a crybaby. It was just that losing her purse was the last straw. She just couldn't take it anymore. She was so tired. It would take forever to make that money back. But her aunt's check could be replaced, at least, although it would probably take some time. Her money was gone for good.

Jordan watched as she turned from him. She was devastated over her purse. "What was in it?"

She didn't answer at first. But then she rolled onto her back. She could feel the tears falling, but she couldn't seem to stop them. "Five hundred dollars. I was supposed to go to the bank, but I forgot."

He watched as she began to cry earnestly. For the first time in a long time, he felt guilty for being so abrasive. Five hundred dollars was a lot of money to lose, especially to someone who didn't have much. Looking down at Samantha, he had a feeling five hundred might as well have been five thousand. He watched helplessly as she rolled back towards the fire. There was nothing either of them could do about it right now. Only a fool would voluntarily wander around in a snowstorm.

Instead, he sat down next to her and rubbed her back to comfort her, though she hardly seemed aware. It didn't take long before Samantha fell asleep. Listening to her talk confirmed what he had already guessed. She was sick. He didn't have anything to give to her. Right now, sleep was the best thing for her.

He yanked off his sweater. He was warm enough now that the turtleneck he was wearing was enough. He looked around the cabin. He had enough food and water for the two of them. He had plenty of firewood, since he'd anticipated the need for it. They would be fine until he could get a tow truck. Then he remembered what Samantha had said about her car. If it were broken down, it would need to be taken to a shop. But she'd lost a good chunk of money tonight, and he'd bet she didn't have the money to fix her car.

That was something he could take care of. He had plenty of money, despite what his father seemed to think. Jordan wasn't always one for charitable donations, but he felt oddly responsible for the woman he'd rescued tonight. He doubted she'd fight him over it. She would be grateful to him for fixing it. Besides, his own truck probably had some damage done to it, and his insurance would pay to fix his truck. And since he hit her, her car would be taken care of. She never even had to know that he fixed her car for her.

Jordan climbed into bed with her. It wasn't that late, but he was tired. It was no wonder, what with the trudge through the snow with Samantha on his shoulder and his earlier ordeal with his father. His dad always made him tired. He shifted to get more comfortable, and he felt her stir beside him.

"What are you doing?" Samantha had felt the bed dip beside her. She'd realized she had drifted off for a few minutes, but she was awake again.

"Going to sleep. You should too, Sam."

She heard him shorten her name, but she couldn't bring herself to correct him. No one shortened her name. But she liked the way it sounded coming from him, his voice deep and almost caressing when he said it. She rolled over to look at him. His eyes were closed. Remembering what he'd done for her, she figured he must be very tired. "How far did you carry me?"

He opened one eye. "Not far. You passed out only a few yards from my driveway."

She tried to remember. "I don't remember there being any homes on this road."

That had been the reason he'd built the cabin where it was. He had wanted privacy. "It's not been here long, and it's not visible from the road."

A vague memory tugged at Samantha, but she couldn't seem to latch onto it. It didn't seem important anyway, so she let it go. "I do want to thank you."

He closed his eyes and took a deep breath. "You would have done the same."

Not likely, she thought. While she would have tried to help him, she certainly couldn't carry him. Samantha dragged her eyes from his broad chest when she realized she was admiring it and looked up at his face again. His skin was tanned, and his blond hair was falling into his eyes. Those eyes were closed now, but she remembered the odd shade of amber. He had friendly eyes, despite his somewhat grim appearance. It was why she hadn't been frightened when she'd woken up alone with him. His shaggy hair and smiling face while he talked to his mother had assured her that he wasn't going to harm her.

Samantha curled up but didn't turn back over. The fire on her back felt good, and watching the man in front of her made her feel relaxed. He was tall; she could tell even while he was lying down. Everyone seemed much taller than she was, but he was probably over six feet tall. And she could tell he was strong. The blanket hugged his legs, revealing the strong line of them. His chest was broad, and his shoulders were wide. She looked up and realized he was watching her. She blushed a bit at having been caught staring at him.

"What are you thinking?" He had seen her staring blindly at his chest. He was afraid she was getting worse.

"I was thinking that it was a good thing that you aren't a weakling." She blushed again at her absurd statement, but he didn't seem to mind because he chuckled.

"Meaning you're grateful that I was strong enough to

carry you through the snow?"

Yes, that was a good explanation for her blatantly staring at, or rather admiring, him. "Yes. I was thinking about that. I would have frozen if you hadn't found me. I don't think I was in the snow very long, but I was freezing when I woke up."

"Are you cold now?"

She was, but she bet it was the fever. "I'm fine." Her head still hurt, but it felt wonderful to be lying down. Her chest hurt, but she remembered the cold air hurting it more. All in all, she was sick, but she was okay. She just needed to sleep. But though she was tired, her mind didn't want to turn off. Something about him was still nagging at her.

He looked down at her. She was huddled under the covers. She was shivering, but he doubted she realized it. He lifted a hand to her forehead. She pulled back a little way from his touch, but other than that didn't move. "You have a fever. I wish I had something to give you, but I don't."

This time instead of pulling away, she pressed her hot forehead deeper into his cool hand, unable to feel embarrassment at the closeness of their bodies, and her unconsciously intimate movement as she rolled slightly closer to him. "It's okay. I've had this fever for a few days now. I passed out in the snow because I was sick. I should have stayed home, but I had to work today."

"How long have you been ill?" He didn't think that this cold was just a few days old.

She ignored his question and pulled the blanket higher. She'd been sick way too long. If it was bad enough that she fainted, she should go to the doctor. She wasn't going to admit it, and she didn't want to hear this man lecture her about her health. When Kitty found out, she would do the lecturing for him.

Abruptly, Samantha realized she had no idea what his name was. He knew hers. That was what was bothering her. "Excuse me?"

Jordan opened his eyes again. He wasn't sleeping but had hoped that if she thought he was, she would go to sleep. Protective instincts he didn't know he had were leaping to the fore. "Go to sleep, Sam."

"That's the problem. I can't sleep because I don't know your name. You seem to know mine."

He realized that he hadn't told her. Introductions seemed unnecessary. It was a strange sensation, but he felt like he already knew her. "I read your name tag."

"Do you have one I could read?" She asked when he didn't answer her question. She shifted onto her elbow.

He pulled her elbow back down. He reached over and grabbed a pillow that had been left behind. He tucked it under her head. "My name is Jordan. Now go to sleep."

She pulled the pillow further under her head and closed her eyes. "Goodnight, Jordan."

He watched as she closed her eyes and relaxed. "Goodnight, Sam."

Jordan watched her drift off to sleep. He rolled onto his back and stared at the ceiling. He wasn't tired anymore. The light from the fire was waltzing across the wooden beams. He watched the patterns dance across the ceiling.

All in all, this had been one of his stranger vacations.

He'd been all over the world during his time in the Navy and his two years as a photographer. People called him, probably for lack of a better word, edgy both back in the Navy and now. Jordan ignored them, but he couldn't help but wonder what this woman would think of him. He glanced at Sam sleeping quietly beside him. He wondered what she'd think when she woke up in the morning. She had the look of a small town girl. This was probably the small town she grew up in. She would know who he was once she stopped and thought about it.

He almost wished she wouldn't. He was never comfortable being a Forrester. During his years in the Navy, he had felt blessed that no one cared who he was or where he'd come from. The men he'd worked with cared about their jobs and their survival. Being a Forrester paled in comparison to being a naval officer. Jordan sometimes wondered if he should have stayed in the Navy. He'd been up for another promotion when he'd quit. But the land he saw during his travels called to him. The men had teased him for carrying his camera around with him. They didn't understand why he didn't make use of the bars and willing women when they were off duty. Bars didn't interest him much. And oftentimes neither did the women. The women he had met during his eleven-year stint in the Navy were varied, and he did enjoy their company when he chose to. He enjoyed women. He liked the way they felt. He liked the way they smelled. But more times than not, he spent his leave time behind his camera lens.

The woman next to him didn't seem like the women he'd known on his travels. She was too sick to care where she was or who she was in bed with. He wondered if she were well, if she'd be interested in the man beside her, or if she'd run from him, though he thought maybe he had caught a brief gleam of interest in her eyes. He was a foot taller than she was and outweighed her considerably. She was so much smaller than he was, and half his weight. He could crush her and not mean to.

Jordan smiled wryly at the direction of his thoughts. He was lusting after a woman he'd met only an hour before. She was sick and pale. Her hair was a tangled mess and looked dull in the light. Her eyes were dark blue, but they were mostly glazed over. She'd had moments of lucidity, but she had gone back to confused quickly. Her body was too thin for his tastes, and he preferred his women taller. She was too small for him.

His body didn't seem to be getting the message his brain was sending out. Whoever she was, she was off limits. He had rescued her from the snow, and she was his responsibility. He was supposed to take care of her and see her safely home. Seducing a young woman was not his usual line, either. He liked older women. Sam was a woman, but she hadn't been one for long.

And she probably had a boyfriend. He could picture the type of man she'd pick. He would be of medium height and build. She'd prefer a man smaller than he himself was. She'd choose the company of a male her own age, one she had more in common with than she would with a man like him. They would enjoy going to the movies together and going out to eat at cheap restaurants. They probably would spend the evening watching television before retiring for the night. Then they'd have boring, uninspired sex.

Jordan's jaw clenched at the thought of another man's hands on Sam. Then he chastised himself. Who she dated and whom she slept with was none of his business. By tomorrow she'd be out of his cabin and out of his life. She'd go back to her job and her boring boyfriend.

He rolled over, putting his back to her, a bit bemused by his interest in her. He was tired. He'd not dated for a while. That was reason enough. The last woman he had dated for more than a month had been over a year ago. The last woman he had slept with had been four months ago, if not longer. He was probably just feeling lonely for female companionship. Samantha was not the woman for him. Small town girls never were. They dreamed of roses and candlelight. They wanted to be charmed and wooed. He didn't have those things in him. If he did try to find himself a wife, she'd have to accept the fact that he wasn't a romantic. His parents' marriage had lasted because they both got out of it what they wanted. They loved each other in their own way, and he was sure they shared much affection for each other. But love was not what held them together; it was a shared desire to maintain their lifestyle and social standing.

Love wasn't something he wanted his marriage to be based on, either, and women raised like Sam expected it. They thought so long as you loved the other person that everything would work out. Jordan knew better. His parents' marriage was what he wanted. He wanted affection from a wife, but he didn't need one who whined when she didn't get what she wanted. He didn't want a woman who cried when she didn't get her every wish. His wife would be a partner, someone who shared his interests and desires. They would manage well together because they shared common goals, not because they shared a bunch of romantic notions that wouldn't see them through the hard times.

His mother called him unromantic. He knew she was right. She said that he had to be in control all the time. She said no woman would tolerate him for very long, whether she loved him or not. She was wrong. Jordan had met many women who fit his criteria for a wife and would have tolerated his precarious moods. He just had lost interest in them too quickly. He wanted a woman with a bit of spirit, but not too much. He was the one who would control the relationship, but he saw no reason it wouldn't work if the woman was willing. His father ultimately had control over his family. It was what Jordan had fought against all these years.

He liked to think that he'd be flexible enough to allow his own children to follow their own paths. But his wife would not be like his sisters. He wouldn't tolerate his wife trying to control him as his sister Lillian did her husband. His brother-in-law didn't care that his sister bossed him around. He had control over the Forrester business empire and that's all he cared about. Amelia wouldn't marry anytime soon because she went through too many men to commit. Her affairs were legendary around here. Jordan didn't expect his wife to be virginal, but she had better not have slept with half the town like Amelia.

Jordan looked over his shoulder when Samantha shifted in her sleep. He didn't know why he was thinking about marriage, probably because his father had mentioned it that evening. With this woman lying trustingly beside him, he couldn't help but wonder about her. In the morning, he told himself, she wouldn't be half as intriguing as she was now. She was a mystery, and once he solved it, he'd lose interest in her like he always did. Content with his assessment, he went to sleep.

* * *

Samantha woke to something wet on her face. She turned her head deeper into the pillow. She mumbled into the pillow. "Vivian, go play."

When a masculine laugh sounded in her ear, her head twisted, and her eyes shot open. In front of her was the ugliest orange tabby she'd ever seen. The cat was sniffing her face. It had been the nose and whiskers she'd felt. Behind her, pressed against her back, was a very warm, very large presence. Memory came back in an instantaneous rush.

"I don't think he liked being called Vivian." Jordan watched as the cat slapped at the loose strands of Samantha's hair. In the sunlight, he could see red in the thick brown mass.

She rolled onto her back and scooted away while she watched wide-eyed as Jordan leaned over her to push the cat away. Having a half-naked man practically on top of her on a bright morning was a bit too much for her frazzled brain. He had obviously removed his turtleneck during the night. She hoped he was wearing pants. She wasn't sure she could deal with a completely nude man in her bed.

Jordan couldn't help feeling pleased when her eyes widened at the contact of their bodies. He was testing her, seeing how she'd respond. She looked ready to faint, and that was not the reaction he was looking for. He grabbed the cat and went back to his side of the bed.

Samantha's small burst of energy failed her. She closed her eyes. Now that she had the chance to sleep, her body was taking over and it wanted more. In the back of her mind, she knew she should stay awake and alert. She was alone with a stranger. She was just so tired that drumming up some concern was too much effort.

"You might as well go back to sleep. There's about two feet of snow on the ground, and the plows won't be by anytime soon."

Samantha opened her eyes and weakly propped herself up on her elbows. "I have to work tonight."

Jordan pushed her back down, his eyes narrowed. "You're not going anywhere. Your car is in a ditch, and my truck is right behind it. The tow trucks won't be able to get out here today. More snow is predicted for this afternoon."

Samantha started to struggle under the large hands that held her down, but he was too strong. "You can't tell me what to do."

Jordan, unable to believe what he was hearing, leaned closer. "I can. I did. You're not going anywhere. You can call your boss and explain to him where you are and what happened. Right now, even if it were a sunny summer day, you wouldn't be leaving. You collapsed in the snow last night, in case you've forgotten. You need to get some sleep.

I'll see to it that you get some."

He was right. Her chest still hurt, and her head was pounding. There wasn't anything she could do if she was snowed in. Her purse was long gone. Her car was dead on the road.

Suddenly, she remembered what he'd said about his truck. She could see a faint bruise on his forehead. "Your truck is behind my car?"

Jordan sat up and stretched. He got a kick of satisfaction as her bright blue eyes widened and stared at his bare chest. In the middle of the night, he'd woken up way too warm. He'd stoked the fire to keep Samantha warm in case she was still chilled from lying in the snow. He had started sweating not long after. He'd stripped off the shirt but left his bottoms on for modesty's sake, her modesty anyway. His thoughts had gone back to the woman lying beside him and kept him awake half the night. It had been a long time since he'd actually slept with a woman, and he'd decided he might as well enjoy it. She was such a slight thing that she hardly took up any room, but he was aware of every inch of her. His body had been attuned to every change in her breathing and every shift of her body during the night.

As he brushed his hair back, he felt the lump. "Yeah, my truck is behind yours. My insurance company is going to love me. I hit your car."

Samantha could see the bump now that went with the light bruise. She sat up and placed two fingers on the spot. "Do you have a headache? Are you hurt anywhere else? You should see a doctor."

He took her fingers and held them. "I hit my head and

blacked out. It probably was just a daze. I wasn't out for long. My head doesn't even hurt this morning, so I must be fine."

Samantha stilled at the feel of his hand holding her fingers. He was stroking his thumb over her fingers. Just that slight touch, and he made her feel breathless and warm all over. Of course, she was running a fever. She pulled her eyes from his. When she shifted on the bed, it caused a coughing fit.

Jordan placed one arm behind her and eased her back down. This feeling of protectiveness was new for him, and he wasn't sure how to react to it. He was never unsure about women. "Lie down."

Samantha couldn't have argued against his command even if she wanted to. Her chest was hurting now, and her throat was raw. The feel of his warm arm behind her and his body beside hers was a strong lure. When he shifted her head to his chest, she didn't protest. The hair on his chest was soft against her cheek, and in that moment, it felt wonderful. The heat from his body helped fight the chill. She curled one arm to her chest and allowed herself to savor the moment.

Jordan watched as her lashes fluttered closed. He eased both of them down flat. She needed to sleep more than anything else. Since it was all he could offer her at the moment, and all she'd probably accept from him, he held her until her breathing settled into a steady rhythm. He let his hand smooth up and down her back, and she snuggled in closer, as if she were snuggling into a warm blanket. He smiled ruefully. He was getting warmer by the second, and it had nothing to do with the fire.

Samantha aroused him without even trying. It had been years since he had looked at a woman and instantly wanted her. And since she had inspired him to think about love and marriage last night, he was having a hard time controlling his reactions to her. There were women he'd seen who he was interested in, but he hadn't felt the need to stand up and howl like a wolf when he spotted them. Jordan closed his eyes and allowed himself to enjoy her. Painful or not, it was worth it.

Samantha slept for the rest of the morning and well into the afternoon. Jordan finally slipped out of bed when he realized they had to eat. McKinley was rubbing his ankles in agreement. Both males ate and watched the woman sleep.

"What do you think? Should I wake her?" Jordan picked up the cat and scratched his ears. The cat purred in agreement. Jordan took the cat with him. He was probably better off stroking McKinley than Samantha.

He shook her shoulder. "Wake up, honey. You need to eat."

It took a minute before she had the strength to move. Her body felt like lead and her head felt full of cotton. She registered his question the third time he said it. "I'm not hungry."

"I didn't ask." Jordan set the cat down and futilely attempted to brush off the cat hair. "I made soup."

It took Jordan a minute to get Samantha into a sitting position. He knew she had to eat, but he hated forcing her to stay awake. Her limbs were trembling, and she had a hard time holding the cup he'd put the soup in. In the end, he sat behind her to support her while she clutched the mug with two hands. He watched her closely to see if she was doing this on purpose to get him to hold her, but it became painfully clear that this was no act when she dumped the hot soup on her and him.

"Damn." Jordan tossed the soup-covered blanket off the bed and sucked the spot on his hand that was full of broth. He took the cup from Samantha, who was trying to apologize and get off his lap. The feel of her bottom rubbing between his legs caused another round of curses to come out of his mouth. The expletives were much worse than his previous one.

"I'm sorry." Samantha managed to slide to the edge of the mattress. The heat of the fire on her back felt good, so she stayed where she was. "I didn't mean to spill it."

Jordan was still cursing silently. "It's not your fault. I should have fed it to you."

Samantha wasn't sure that was a better solution, but from his standpoint, it probably was. The hot mug had felt good on her chilled hands, but it was his chest against her back that was the best. Sometime while she'd slept, he'd pulled on a black t-shirt and changed into jeans. In deference to the cold floors, he had on a pair of thick gray socks. Still, even with the shirt on, she had a hard time forgetting how he'd looked half naked. Knowing it was inappropriate to be thinking about him in such lustful ways, she kept her eyes on the floor. At the rate she was going, it would be no time at all before she pictured him completely nude, bathed in firelight.

Jordan cleaned up the mess. He watched Sam out of the corner of his eye. She didn't appear worse, but she didn't look any better. "Still hungry? I have some bread I could toast. The electricity is back on, but I don't expect it to last long with the next round of snow coming."

Samantha nodded. She hadn't wanted the soup, but now that she had something in her stomach, she was still hungry. She'd not gotten much of the soup in her mouth; most of it ended up on the blanket. When he handed her a plate, she set it carefully on her lap. She ate the toast gratefully. When he handed her a half glass of juice, she managed it without incident.

Tired again, she just wanted to lie down. Jordan was watching her through slitted eyes. Samantha stifled a yawn. "I hate to be such bad company, but I'm tired."

Jordan came over from where he had been standing. "I'm going to change the sheets and put the mattress back on the bed before you go back to sleep."

Samantha squealed when he lifted her up off the mattress without warning. She clutched at his shoulders as he spun her around. When she felt her backside hit the couch, she let go. Confused by his abrupt movements, she watched silently. Then she watched amazed. He lifted the mattress as if it weighed nothing. She watched the muscles shift in his arms, but he made it look easy. He efficiently remade the bed and dug out another blanket from the closet.

When he came back to pluck her off the couch, she found her voice. "I'm capable of walking."

"I know." He lifted her up and carried her to the bed. Under any other circumstances, he would have followed her down onto the mattress. He pulled the sheet over her and shook out the new blanket. "Warm enough?"

Her voice was raspy when she could finally speak. He'd been looking at her like she was a desirable woman instead of a lump of sick woman. "I'm fine."

Jordan leaned down and brushed a kiss over her soft lips. "Go to sleep."

"You're supposed to kiss me awake, not asleep," Samantha murmured.

He watched as she fell instantly to sleep. "Maybe I will." Jordan turned his back on her and set about straightening up. He washed the dishes and put the blanket in the washer.

He got a kick out of his cabin. In Alaska, he didn't have many amenities. When he'd built this one, he wanted the look of a cabin but all the comforts of a real home. He had a separate bathroom and a large tub and shower. He had a washer and dryer hidden behind double doors and had a fully equipped kitchen. He'd kept the main room open with a couch, a bookcase, a bed, and a radio. The radio was more for weather updates than anything else. It had a battery backup in case of emergency. In keeping with the feel of a cabin, there wasn't a television or a phone. But he didn't want to hand wash his clothes, and he liked to eat. Bathing properly was a luxury, he knew all too well, and he'd gone all out.

Alaska had been good to him. The small cabin he'd bought did have running water. The water heater, however, barely did its job. More times than not, he had a cold shower. For some reason that he could not explain, he had not replaced the cranky heater. The kitchen had a wood-burning stove, and he'd burned more food on it than he'd actually eaten off of it. He'd almost rather have cooked over an open flame. At least he had more control over a campfire than his primitive stove. The stove had been a taciturn piece of equipment when it was made, and it hadn't changed with time.

What amazed him was how much he missed it. He moved around often. In his late twenties, he had decided he would probably never settle down in one place. Then he'd gone to Alaska to photograph the vastness of the frozen state at the beginning of the fall over a year ago. When he'd left Alaska three months earlier, he hadn't taken much with him, realizing that he would return. He'd headed into the Rocky Mountains for a job he'd taken, and he and his camera had had a good time with the snow-covered peaks. He'd decided since he was so close to home, he'd visit. It was only going into the second week of January, so his mother was happy he'd spent at least part of the holidays with them. He'd taken all the pictures he'd wanted, and his cabin was completed on time, so he'd been free to come home. But his idea of home had changed this past year, even though he'd spent so much money building this cabin. Home was becoming another place, a place he certainly never would have considered years ago. His mother would probably have a fit if she knew he was considering moving permanently to Alaska.

He was getting to like the idea of a home base. Since he'd left the Navy two years earlier, he'd been to a few different countries and taken thousands of pictures. He'd been attracted to Alaska, and he'd wanted to capture the sweeping snow and desolation that came after the short summer. What he'd discovered was the richness that Alaska offered.   He'd stayed through the winter, and then photographed the incredible changes brought throughout spring and summer. It wasn't a dead, frozen wasteland to those who looked beneath the surface, though in the dead of winter he couldn't blame people for thinking it. He doubted his family would see it any other way. But he'd not cared what his family thought for over a dozen years now. He was independent; he relied on no one, and no one counted on him for anything.

He supposed at the moment that wasn't entirely true. The woman sleeping contentedly in his bed was a responsibility. He couldn't help but wonder what she'd think of his unprecedented reactions to her. This sense of possessiveness went beyond rational. He felt like he'd known her forever, yet she was a stranger. Whatever happened between now and when he left Colorado, he planned to explore this feeling with the woman who inspired it. His body leapt to attention at the thought. Last night he'd gone from telling himself he couldn't have her to telling himself he couldn't let her leave until he had. He wouldn't be leaving until he'd explored all the possibilities.

Chapter Four

When Samantha woke again, it was dark. At first, she snuggled back down, still feeling tired. Then she realized what the darkness meant. She shot up and looked around for Jordan, not that he was hard to find in the open space of the cabin. He was by the stove.

"Awake?" Jordan didn't have to turn around to know Samantha was awake. He'd become oddly tuned to her.

"I need the phone." She struggled to untwist herself from the blankets. Just the small struggle made her feel weak.

"I called your work for you already. I didn't call your aunt because I don't know her name, so I couldn't look it up." He finished stirring, then set the lid on the pan.

"It's Rose Brody. What did my boss say?" Samantha dropped back down. She didn't like that he had taken it upon himself to call her boss. Her tone must have been clear because he sounded angry when he responded.

"You work for a jerk." He pulled out a knife and began slicing the bread he had bought the day before. "Your last name Brody?"

She gave an exasperated sigh. "Yes, it is. Look, you should have woken me up to call him." She felt the need to defend her decision. She might as well be talking to herself.

"A fire alarm directly in your ear wouldn't have woken you up." He set the knife down and faced Samantha. "Look at you. You're trembling and you've been awake a whole minute. You're not in any position to argue with me. Dinner will be ready soon. Enjoy it. It might be one of the last hot meals you'll get."

"What does that mean?" Samantha had a premonition. She looked out the window. She had a feeling the darkness outside wasn't because of the time of day.

He followed her gaze. "My guess is that we'll have another half a foot or so. The weatherman is predicting some strong winds. You know this area as well as I do. The power will be out tonight. It will be a small miracle if it doesn't."

"My boss won't have closed." She gave him a direct look when his face took on a pinched demeanor.

"Forget it. You're not going anywhere unless you feel like walking." He set up a tray and arranged a meal for Samantha.

She wanted to argue, but she held her tongue. There was no point in making Jordan angry, and he was right. She couldn't go anywhere. "I have to call my aunt."

"No problem. You can eat first, then call her. After that, I suggest a bath. You might as well enjoy the hot water while you can."

Samantha noticed that his hair was damp. She'd slept through his shower and dinner preparations. She saw they were having soup again. This looked fresh. "Did you make this?"

"Don't sound so shocked. I lived in northern Alaska for almost a year. I arrived last winter during the beginning of the winter season. I ate a lot of hot soup to keep warm. I got sick of the canned stuff, so I started making it myself.

I've got tons of it frozen in containers. Hot soup and fresh bread." He set the tray down.

"I promise not to spill it this time." The soup smelled wonderful. There were a dozen different vegetables floating in the thick broth. The rice made it filling.

They ate in silence. Jordan watched to make sure she could handle the spoon. The way her hand was shaking, he had doubts, but she managed to eat the bowl of soup and the bread. He fixed himself another bowl and ate by the fire.

Samantha waited until Jordan was finished eating before she asked for the phone. The call to her aunt was stilted. She knew it was best to get the bad news out of the way. She knew Jordan could hear her aunt's tirade from across the cabin. Samantha let her yell out her upset at the lost money. Afterwards, Samantha said she would see her as soon as the snow was plowed enough to allow her through. Rose was furious that she'd be missing so much work, but even Rose couldn't get out of the driveway at the moment, so she wasn't as angry as she would have been had Samantha decided to use her cold as an excuse to stay home.

"I take it she's upset." Jordan eased the phone from her clenched fist.

"I think she might use this as an excuse to move. She's wanted to move for a while now. She has a friend in Washington State who has been trying to get her to move out that way for some time now. My aunt was trained as a legal secretary, but she hasn't worked in a law office in years. Anyway, she says she's tired of struggling. She wants to move and go back to what she calls a real job. Vivian doesn't care."

"Whose Vivian? You called my cat Vivian this morning." Said cat was lying in front of the fireplace. Jordan handed her a glass of juice.

"My younger sister. She's five." Samantha smiled wryly into her juice. "She likes to wake me up in the mornings."

"Does your aunt have custody of your sister?" Jordan figured her parents were dead.

"My aunt is her mother. My father married my mom's sister after my mom died, and they had Vivian together. It was why Rose agreed to the marriage in the first place."

"So your aunt married your father so she could have a child of her own?" Jordan figured it was as good a reason as any other he'd heard.

"Yes. My dad wanted someone to take care of me. He got tired of paying a housekeeper to watch me while he was away." Samantha saw the question and answered it. "He drove a truck cross country."

"Where's your dad now?" Somehow, he knew he was gone.

"Don't know. He divorced my aunt when I turned eighteen. He let her have the house and all the possessions. It didn't amount to much. He stuck around only long enough to see Vivian born before he took off. We got letters on occasion; then they stopped altogether about a year after the divorce." Samantha yawned, unable to help herself.

"Am I boring you?" he teased. "I'll go run your bathwater."

The bath felt good. She somehow managed to get the strength to wash her hair along with her body. Her scalp was starting to itch. That and the thought of the power being out again motivated her enough to get it done. It would take forever for her hair to dry, but right now she didn't care. She looked at the clothes Jordan had given her and her sadly wrinkled uniform. The uniform needed a wash now that she'd slept in it for a day. The pants were okay, but her underwear wasn't. She leaned over and grabbed them. They had to be washed if she was going to wear them again.

"Are you okay in there?" Jordan's voice called through the door.

"Fine." She managed to wring out her underwear and hang it over the towel rack. She tossed the bra in the water to wash as well. "Can I borrow a shirt?"

Samantha heard a mumble and a chuckle. She wrapped the towel around herself. It was big enough to go around almost twice. He apparently believed in comfort. She grabbed the rest of her clothes. She jumped a bit at the knock on the door, then got a grip on herself. She opened the door wide enough to take the clothes.

"A shirt and a fresh pair of pants." He didn't bother to disguise his interest. Her shoulders were bare and creamy. Her hair hung wet and loose around them. Her eyes looked huge in her face as she watched him peruse her body. He wasn't surprised when she hurriedly shut the door. Either way, it was too late. He'd seen the tops of her surprisingly full breasts framed by the white towel she wore. What he could see of her legs was slim and nicely shaped beneath the towel. Her body was flushed pink from her bath. No matter how small, she looked like a woman, a desirable woman.

When she emerged, Jordan had himself under control. She might be desirable, but she was also sick. She was too weak to fend off an advance, and she was too weak to appreciate one if she were interested. Either way, his body had better accept "no" for an answer.

"Give me your clothes and I'll wash them." Jordan took the bundle from her. He saw her undergarments hanging in the bathroom. He kept his chuckle to himself when she blushed as he grabbed them. "I'll wash these too."

Samantha nodded, too embarrassed to answer. She had an odd tingling in her belly at the sight of his large hands clutching her underwear. She turned her back on him and decided to sit in a chair for a while. She'd slept more in the last two days than she had in weeks.

"Tired of the bed?" Jordan was drying his hands as he came back into the main room. "You look like a kid in those clothes."

Samantha glanced down. "I always look like a kid."

Jordan disagreed. "No. You may be small, but you don't look like a child. How old are you?"

Samantha pursed her lips. "Twenty-two. At the moment, I feel a lot older."

"That's because you're sick. Once you're feeling better, you'll be back to your old self." Jordan was silent for a minute. Then he shrugged his shoulders. "I have a sister a year younger than you. She still acts like a child."

Samantha looked up from the fire. Blond hair, a new cabin, and a sister a year younger. "Good heavens, you're Jordan Forrester."

His eyebrows rose at the dismay he heard in her voice.

"So? You knew that."

"No, I did not. You just said your name was Jordan." Samantha's eyes didn't leave his face. It was as if she were facing a stranger.

"What's the big deal? I know you're from around here. I assumed you knew who I was. There aren't that many Jordans around here, and this is a small town." He was confused by her tone; a small surge of anger filled him at the way she was studying him. Gone was the hint of interest he'd seen in her eyes, replaced by what he thought might be suspicion.

"I didn't know. Kitty told me you were in town the other day and that you'd built a cabin, but it never occurred to me to think you were him."

"You make me sound like a criminal." Jordan rose. He picked Samantha up from her chair and gently dumped her back on the bed. "You apparently need more sleep."

She tried to sit up, but he pushed her back down. She didn't fight the almost steady pressure of his hand; her body was now filled with tension.

"What is the matter with you? You've been here for a day and now you decide I'm dangerous? It's a bit late for caution. Shut up and go to sleep." Jordan turned his back on her and went to clean up the mess he'd made. Dinner seemed like a long time ago.

Samantha bit her lip at the anger she'd just witnessed. She didn't understand why she'd reacted the way she had, and she certainly hadn't meant to insult him. She just didn't like the thought that he was "Jordan Forrester" and not just Jordan, the man who rescued her. The Forresters were a notorious bunch; at least the kids were rumored to be. Gossip floated about the family. Some stories were outlandish, although those centered on the youngest daughter. Others were quite believable, such as the rumors of possible corruption during his father's political years. She supposed the rumors could be exaggerated. They were the only wealthy family in the area, and she supposed that a lot of the rumors could have been made up out of spite. Jordan was the one unknown entity in the family. He was the one people knew nothing about past his school years. Rumors of his time spent in the Navy were the most rampant. Some of the more outrageous rumors reported he'd been in the Special Forces Unit, embarking on dangerous, secretive missions for the government. Samantha didn't know much about the Navy, but Jordan looked like he could be dangerous. Looking at his broad shoulders and long tapered legs, she knew that it wasn't outside the realm of possibility. There was a controlled power to his body that was lacking in other men. That didn't necessarily make him dangerous to her, but now that she knew who he was, it made her wary of him.

Samantha continued studying him while his back was to her. His hair was long for a Navy man, but then again, he'd retired two years before, if the rumors were right. He had said he'd spent the last year in Alaska. There were military bases in Alaska. She wondered if he was retired or not. She supposed it didn't matter. He was still in good shape. He'd carried her through the snow, not an easy feat in a blizzard, no matter who you were. He'd sustained a head injury and had no side effects. He probably could have carried her ten times the distance and still had energy left over.

"Are you finished appraising me?" Jordan's angry voice assailed her ears.

"I was wondering if you were still in the Navy," she said honestly.

He took a calming breath. "No. I quit two years ago. I decided I wanted out. Any other questions?"

"Were you really in the Special Forces?" She should have bitten her lip, but she really wanted to know.

He turned to her. His eyes were flat, the earlier humor gone. "No. I enlisted and did my job. Then I quit."

When he didn't elaborate, she bit her lip. This was something he obviously didn't want to talk about. "I'm sorry I reacted the way I did."

"Forget it. I obviously have a reputation that precedes me." He tossed the hand towel and reined in his emotions. He was losing control of his temper. He knew he had one. It had gotten him in trouble over the years. It was one of the biggest reasons he'd joined the Navy. He wanted to learn self-control. He had learned it, but it still sometimes failed him. This woman's accusatory gaze set him off.

"I am sorry." Samantha's voice softened. "I didn't mean to sound so suspicious. I suppose I should be flattered. I'll have such a story to tell of how I was rescued by the notorious Jordan Forrester."

Jordan took another calming breath. When he turned to her, she was smiling at him. "Going to tell everyone about your dramatic rescue?"

"Just Kitty. She saw you at the grocery store the other day. She has a crush on you. Her husband would be upset if he found out, so she keeps it a secret." Samantha stifled another yawn.

"Who's Kitty?" He wanted to keep her talking. Now that he'd calmed down, he was enjoying watching her stammer through the conversation.

"I work with her. Her real name is Katherine Lawson, but she insists on being called Kitty."

"Tall, with blond spiky hair? She's old enough to be my mother." Jordan pulled a chair up closer to the bed.

"Maybe, technically, she's old enough, but she'd have been in high school. She'll be fifty this year. How do you know her?" Samantha rolled onto her side and bunched the pillow under her head.

"You get to know people in passing. I don't know her well, but I know her husband. He owns the hardware store. He got a lot of business through me this past year."

"The cabin, right?" Samantha's eyes closed.

"Yes, the cabin. I bought most of the materials through him. Despite his small operation, he managed to get some good deals on the materials I needed. It was a good thing, too. I sunk most of my money into this place." Jordan pulled the blanket higher over her shoulder.

"Most of your money? Not to be rude, but the Forresters are supposed to be very wealthy, and this place isn't exactly a mansion." Samantha opened her eyes to see his face.

"My father is wealthy. My grandfather is wealthy. I suppose that makes my oldest sister and her husband wealthy. The problem with being a Forrester is that you're only rich if you work for the company. I don't work for the company, so I don't get a share of it."

"You're not rich?" Samantha watched him watching her.

"You almost sound happy about it. No, I'm not rich." He wasn't rich, but he wasn't destitute either. He didn't tell Samantha that. If she thought him poor, that was fine with him. He didn't want her to be interested in him for his money.

"I don't know that I'm happy about it. I just thought that the whole family had a lot of money. The rumors say you are." Samantha closed her eyes again, content to listen to the low timbre of his voice.

"I can imagine what the rumors say. I suppose the family is what you'd consider wealthy. When my father dies, I suppose I'll inherit something. Lillian and her husband ran the family empire. They'll inherit it. Amelia will probably inherit a considerable amount because she's the baby of the family and female. My father has some old-fashioned ideas about women."

"Old-fashioned? Meaning he thinks she needs to be taken care of because she can't do it herself?" Samantha heard an odd note in his voice.

"Yeah. I get some of my old-fashioned ideas from him." It was a warning to her that he held many of the same opinions. He wasn't as extreme as his father. He didn't think women should be handed everything their heart's desired. He'd seen what that did to his youngest sister. But he did believe that a man should take care of and protect the woman he marries. It was just another reason why he hadn't wanted to get married before. He would have to take care of her and protect her. He hadn't met a woman who he thought deserved his protection.

He silently chuckled at his own arrogance. If his mother heard his thoughts, she would have boxed his ears. She was very independent and fought his father's controlling ways. She'd tried to raise him thinking that men and women were completely equal. He bought the equality part. Men and women were equal. He didn't think women should be subservient. He did believe that in a relationship each person had their role. He didn't think a woman should clean up after him or wait on him hand and foot. He did expect her to allow him to make the difficult decisions in their lives when needed. He wanted her to understand that he would never harm her and would only do what was best for his family. His mother didn't understand that. She said that was chauvinistic. So be it.

"Samantha?" Jordan watched her lashes flutter open. "Just seeing if you were awake."

"Not really." Samantha snuggled down into the covers. "I like listening to your voice."

It was the second time she'd hinted at the growing intimacy between them. Both times she was half asleep. She'd done it yesterday when she'd mentioned his kissing her awake. Now she hinted at it by admitting to being pleased by his presence. He kept up a light conversation while she fell asleep. When he was sure she was deeply asleep, he rose and put the chair back.

She interested him both mentally and physically. He wondered if she felt the same way. It was a useless exercise, thinking about it. But as he undressed and slid into bed with her, he couldn't help but think about what it would be like to have her permanently in his bed.

* * *

Samantha woke up the next morning to a cat in her ear. It seemed like he was going to be her alarm clock while she was here. She batted the tabby away, and he heeded the warning. She hadn't seen much of the cat during the day yesterday; of course, she had been asleep for most of it. He apparently liked to venture out in the morning and hide all day.

"McKinley likes you." Jordan adjusted his position on the bed, bringing a suddenly reluctant Samantha back into his arms. She'd worked her way onto his shoulder during the night, with a little assistance. He liked the feel of her soft cheek on his shoulder and her warm breath on his chest. All down the side of his body, she was pressed against him, her breasts flattened along his torso, and one of her thighs draped around his legs.

Samantha stared at the dark blond hair tapering across the expanse of his broad chest. The long fingers of his opposite hand were wrapped around her shoulder, bringing her flush against him. His other arm was underneath the pillow that was now under his head instead of hers. He might be used to having women plastered to him, but she wasn't used to being the woman. The only thing she snuggled up with at night was her quilt. She could feel his leg that was under her thigh. It was bare. She swallowed convulsively, and part of her tried to pretend this wasn't happening. The other part was relishing the closeness, her skin tingling where it met his.

"McKinley?" Her voice sounded too deep and husky.

"The cat. I picked him up in Alaska when I was shooting Mount McKinley. It seemed fitting." Jordan rolled a bit more onto his side, bringing their bodies face to face.

"I must be more tired than I thought. You were shooting Mount McKinley?" Samantha wedged her arms between them, intending to put some distance between their bodies.

"Pictures, Sam. I'm a photographer." Jordan didn't mind her hands on his chest one bit. He shifted position, allowing her better access but not allowing her to move away.

"Why do you call me Sam?" Samantha was frowning. He managed to bring them closer together despite her arms. If she wanted to, she had access to his chest. The sight of a male nipple this close to her face first thing in the morning was disconcerting. What was worse was that she wanted to touch.

"I like it. Samantha is very formal, and Sammy is too immature." Jordan grabbed her body under her arms and tugged her higher up on the bed.

"Jordan, don't." Her mouth was level with his, and she knew he was going to kiss her.

"Don't call you Sam?" His lips nuzzled hers and he enjoyed the way her breath released in a rush against his mouth. He'd been wanting to do this for an hour since he woke up.

"Yes. I mean, no. Don't kiss me. You shouldn't." Samantha turned her face, knowing she should, but she didn't turn it far enough.

He traced her lips lightly with the tip of his tongue. "Do you have a boyfriend?"

Samantha shivered helplessly in his grasp. His free hand was smoothing up and down the side of her body, the palm of his hand brushing the side of her breast. His other arm was under her side and around her back, arching her body toward his.

"Do you, Sam?" Not that it mattered. He wanted her, and he wasn't going to share.

"No." She released another breath she was holding and gave up. She lifted her face for better access to his mouth. He had the softest, sweetest-tasting mouth.

With her acquiescence, Jordan took her mouth completely, bringing her as close to him as their position would allow. "Wrap your arms around me, Sam."

Samantha obeyed. She felt his body twist again and she was on her back, his large body pressing her into the mattress. He lay half on, half off. Her breasts were crushed against the weight of his chest, but her legs were free.

"You taste good in the morning." Jordan's words were mumbled against her lips as he urged her mouth open. When she obeyed his command, he swept into the territory behind her teeth. She whimpered into his mouth. He wanted her to. He wanted her writhing under him.

Samantha lost all sense of herself. Never had she felt these sensations with another man. The boys she'd dated in high school had not even an ounce of the expertise Jordan was showing her. Jordan knew exactly how to move his mouth; he knew exactly the right angle. His kisses weren't wet and sloppy. They were moist and arousing.

Jordan figured that at the rate they were going, he'd have her naked and open within minutes. His body was throbbing painfully against his boxers. He'd stripped the night before, keeping only his boxers on. He hadn't thought she'd appreciate waking up with a naked man. In some ways, they were still strangers, though she knew more about him than most. But with her body arching under his and her mouth open and mobile, he didn't think she minded his nudity.

Samantha felt his fingers on the buttons of the shirt she was wearing. Since it was his shirt, he had it open to her waist in no time. He left the two bottom buttons fastened as he stripped it from her shoulders, baring her naked breasts to his gaze. She wasn't sure when his mouth had left hers, but her lips were throbbing and swollen, as if his were still there. She watched in a daze as his index finger traced the upper slope of her right breast. When his mouth fastened onto the flesh he was admiring, she became acutely aware that the only thing between them was his underwear and her pants. The fact that she wasn't wearing any underwear became uncomfortably noticeable to her.

Jordan eased his body into the cradle of her legs as she shifted restlessly on the bed. Maybe he overestimated his five-minute estimate. He wanted to strip her bare and take what she was offering. He cupped the breast he had been loving with his mouth and took the other. Her breasts were fuller than he'd expected. They were rounded just perfectly and firm. He liked the feel of them, the size and shape just right for his possession. It seemed Sam agreed with him, for she arched her breast more fully into his mouth.

Samantha felt the pressure of his mouth shift from her breast to her belly, his hands taking up where his mouth left off. Her body was aching and throbbing. She lay helplessly under him, her thighs squeezing his hips. Dear heaven, no man had ever lain between her legs, and the feel of his erection pressing against the softness of her most sensitive flesh made her feel the sweetest pain she'd ever felt.

"Jordan?" His name escaped her lips as his tongue traced across her stomach where the pants met her waist. He was slowly easing the fabric lower, his teeth nibbling and biting little kisses along the way. When his hands worked under the waistband to cup her backside, she knew things had gone too far. The feel of his large hands cradling her lower body as he worked the kisses back up her body forced her to remember where she was and whom she was with. Despite the aching emptiness in her lower body, they had to stop. She wasn't ready to give herself to a man she hardly knew. A lifetime of reservation came to the fore.

Jordan felt the slight stiffening of her body as his fingers clenched her backside. He could feel the dampening of the pants she wore as their bodies were pressed intimately together. But the stiffening of her body wasn't something he could ignore, as much as he wanted to. He didn't want her frightened; he wanted her willing.

"What, Sam?" His fingers slid farther down and cupped the back of her thighs, bringing her even closer to his aroused flesh.

"We can't do this." Samantha felt tears sting her eyes at the feel of his length rubbing up and down between her legs. She didn't know if he was aware of the movements of his body or not. She was highly aware and knew it needed to stop while she could still think clearly. "I can't sleep with you."

Jordan considered stripping the pants down and showing her for the liar she was. Her breasts were still full and erect. The pink flush of her body went from the top of her head to her navel.

"Why, Sam? Why do we need to stop?" Jordan brought his mouth back to hers, his teeth biting her lower lip. "You want me as much as I want you. You've already admitted there is no one else."

Samantha didn't know how to control what she was feeling. Her limbs were trembling again as they had for days, but this had nothing to do with exhaustion. He was right. There was no one else. But there had never been anyone else before him, and she wasn't ready. Things were moving too quickly.

She felt one tear trickle down her cheek, then another. She was hardly aware that she was crying.

Jordan lifted a hand from her thighs to her cheek. He smoothed away a tear. "Why are you crying? I won't hurt you."

Samantha felt his tongue soothing her lower lip where he'd bitten none too gently. Her words were soft because of the tears that were choking her. "It will hurt. I've not done this before. I'm not ready to."

It took Jordan a second to realize what she was saying. Then it dawned on him. "Ah, hell."

It was not the comforting response she wanted. His remark made her tears fall harder. "I'm sorry. I never meant for this to happen."

Jordan rolled from between her thighs and settled his

body alongside hers. He buttoned the shirt back up, then pulled her back into his arms and pressed her cheek against him so that her head was cradled under his chin. She only struggled for a second before she settled down.

"I forget how young you are." Jordan knew Amelia wasn't still a virgin, but his sister Lillian had been until she'd married at twenty-four. Samantha was only twenty-two. She was a small-town girl, born and raised. He should have known. Now that his body was calming down, he realized how unskilled her kisses had been. She hadn't even touched him as he had been touching her. Her fingers had clenched around his shoulders and hadn't moved unless he did the moving.

"Are you mad at me?" Samantha wasn't sure he heard her quiet question. She wasn't sure she wanted an answer.

It took a minute before he replied. "No. I'm not mad. I'm still horny, but I'll survive."

She could tell that he was. She was so much shorter than he was, and she could feel him against her hip. She probably should be embarrassed and move away, but she wanted to stay where she was. He wasn't stroking her body now, just holding her still. She could feel his chest rising and falling under her own. Only one breast was smashed against him this time, but it felt good. He felt good.

"I guess I took you by surprise." Jordan shifted his position, trying to ease the lower half of his body away from her. At the rate he was going, it was going to take all day to relax.

"I suppose it didn't help that I was lying on top of you." Samantha kept her voice low, not wanting to disturb the peace she felt.

Jordan chuckled at that. "You had some help."

She felt as much as heard his amusement. "Did I?"

"Mmm." Jordan kissed the top of her head, then slid out of bed. "Are you hungry?"

Samantha blinked at the quick change of topic. But now that he mentioned it, she was. "Very."

"We're going to have to be imaginative. The electricity went out last night about eleven. We have another foot of snow to add to the last two feet. Both our vehicles are buried, and we aren't going anywhere until it stops snowing."

It was Tuesday. She shook her head as if to clear it. "I can't believe I've slept for almost two days."

Jordan kept his back to her. Every time he watched her sleep, he got ticked off. She was so run down her body had given out on her. He was grateful that her cough seemed to have lessened and that her fever was gone. She still sounded congested and nasally, but sleep had done her a world of good. Her aunt should have tied her to her bed and made her stay in it. His feelings toward the unknown woman were getting more hostile the longer he was with Sam. She was probably a lot thinner than she should be. Her waist was so tiny his hands could almost span it. Her face had hollows that probably weren't supposed to be there, either. The bruising under her eyes had mostly disappeared, but he remembered how dark they had been just two days earlier. All in all, her aunt had a lot to answer for.

Jordan left the room, leaving Samantha to stare after him. His legs were long and muscular. His calves and thighs were thick, spattered with the same dark blond hair that covered his chest. His back was broader than she realized. The definition of his muscles was noticeable, even in the faint morning light. His shoulders tapered into a narrower waist; the line of his spine just begged to be traced by a woman's fingers. As her gaze drifted farther down, she tried not to stare at the fit of his boxers, but it was useless.

When he disappeared from her sight, she rolled over onto her stomach. Jordan Forrester was dangerous. She doubted there was a woman alive who could resist him. As Samantha buried her face in the pillow that smelled like the man who'd just vacated the bed, she knew she was in trouble.

Chapter Five

"Are you really a photographer?" Samantha asked the question that had been plaguing her as she took another bite of the apple Jordan had sliced up for her. Ever since he'd mentioned it, she'd been wondering about it. She'd never met a professional photographer before.

"I am. I got into it while I was in the Navy. I was at all these different places, and I wanted to keep them in my memory. I bought a book on photography. I was hooked after my first day."

"Do you sell your work? I mean, you said you don't have any of your family's money, so do you support yourself with your pictures?"

She looked so sweet and adorable curled up on his bed, with her auburn hair tumbled around her shoulders from his fingers, and her mouth still red and swollen from his kisses. Jordan couldn't help but be drawn into the conversation, though he'd rather talk about her. "I do pretty well. I was able to buy a place in Alaska, in addition to building this place. My parents ask me the same question every time I visit. They think I've been starving and living in a slum."

Samantha tucked the blanket closer around her legs and shifted into a more comfortable position. She'd started this conversation to break the tension. She was still feeling horribly embarrassed by what had almost happened in this very bed just half an hour before. He'd gone about making breakfast as if nothing had happened. Maybe as far as he was concerned, nothing had. She was trying not to dwell on it.

She had asked him about being a photographer to break the ice, but now she really wanted to know. "Did you take lots of pictures of Alaska? How cold is it really?"

Jordan set another plate in her lap. He'd boiled an egg for her over the fire. The toast was a barely edible mess, but the egg was fine.

"It's very cold," Jordan said solemnly. Then he ruined it by smiling. "At first, I couldn't believe how cold it was. I was accustomed to living in much warmer climates. In the southern half of the state, it can be pretty warm, but I didn't spend any time there. The further north you go, the colder it gets. You get used to it. The cabin I bought is much more rustic than this place. Everything is run by gas, and the tank is so old it leaks. There is running water, but it's a pain to heat, and the pipes froze a couple times. I could do some remodeling to bring it up to date, but I made do with it as it is."

Something in his tone made Samantha interrupt. "You want to go back. Why did you build this cabin if you don't really want to live here?"

She'd summed him up fast, he realized. It amazed him how in tune the two of them were. "I did it mostly because I love my family, but I hate living with them. This way, I can visit as much as I like, but I can escape when I need to. My grandfather was the one who suggested the cabin. My father was resigned, and my mother argued it was a waste of money up until the last nail was hammered. She's okay with it now, but I'm waiting for her to argue that I'd better install a phone. She'll find something else to worry about after that."

Samantha had a hard time visualizing the rest of his family members. His sister was the only member she knew, and if the others were like her, she didn't want to meet them. They certainly wouldn't approve of her sleeping with their son. Not that she planned on doing that. But after what had happened between them, Samantha's curiosity about Jordan and his family had increased. He was no longer some vague member of their community. He was a living, breathing, very male presence in her subconscious now. For as long as she lived, she would never be able to listen to gossip about him and be able to picture him as anything other than the man he was.

"Anyway, I don't see being able to spend much time in the cabin for a while," Jordan said, oblivious to Samantha's sudden silence. "I'll be heading to Australia in a week or two. I'm not looking forward to spending the end of summer there after being in the cold for so long."

"How long will you stay there?" Samantha felt tired all of a sudden and lay down.

Jordan glanced over at her, his lips pursing at the sight of her once again on her back. "Three months or so. Since I started selling my pictures, I've been staying in one place longer than I did back in the Navy. My first pictures were sold to a travel magazine. I wrote a pretty lousy article to go with the pictures. They liked the pictures enough to edit my article and print it. Since then, most of my pictures have been for travel ads or magazines, even books on occasion. The pictures of Australia are for a book. Once I get established, I hope to move on to projects that I have more control over."

"You must be looking forward to it. I've never traveled before." Samantha pulled her knees to her chest as she rolled to her side, but she opened her eyes.

"I like seeing new things. After thirteen years of traveling, I want to settle down a bit. I figured Alaska would afford me plenty of photographic opportunities and a place to live. I imagine I'll still have to travel a lot, but hopefully not for three-month stretches like this next trip will be."

It saddened Samantha that he was leaving so soon. Part of her had hoped to see him again once she left the solitude of his cabin. How silly, she thought, to be weaving any type of fantasy around a man like Jordan. Forrester or not, he was definitely out of her league, destined for great things.

"Samantha?" Jordan watched as her eyes fluttered shut, then opened again.

"What?" Her eyes felt like lead, and she just wanted to sleep again.

"Are you all right?" He came over and sat on the bed beside her.

"Tired."

Jordan didn't like the way she kept drifting in and out of sleep. He wished he knew more about her and how long she'd been sick. But her breathing sounded fine. He didn't think she had pneumonia or bronchitis. "You must be worn out. When was the last time you got a good night's sleep?"

Samantha barely registered the question. She answered

it truthfully when she otherwise would have lied. "Ages. Between work and Vivian, I don't sleep much. We need the money, so I work extra a lot."

That bothered him. "What about your aunt?"

"She works during the day. She's a receptionist for a dentist's office. She works days during the week, and I work evenings. Someone has to be home with Vivian. At least now she's in school for most of the day." Samantha stifled a small cough and then a yawn.

"Go to sleep, baby." Jordan brushed a light kiss on her forehead. Though it wasn't his intention, he noted the normal temperature of her skin. Perhaps she really was just worn out.

"Okay." Samantha rolled onto her stomach and fell asleep.

Jordan sat beside her, rubbing her back as he'd done before. He remembered when he'd first joined the Navy. Basic training wore you out. He and the other men had persevered, finding reserves of energy they hadn't known they had. He remembered days when he was so bone-tired that he hadn't thought he'd make it back to his bunk. Somehow, he had always managed to stay on his feet as long as it was necessary.

The life that Samantha was leading wasn't much different. She found enough energy to stay on her feet. Given the slightest chance, her body had collapsed. He doubted she'd wake again until late this evening. She would be back in bed and sound asleep for the coming night, as well. He hated the thought that she would leave here and go right back to her daily grind, wearing herself out until she collapsed again.

There was nothing he could do. He couldn't take her with him to Australia. He doubted she'd go even if he were able to. She seemed committed to her family and taking care of them as best she could. He admired that in her. He didn't care for weak people who couldn't be depended on. Samantha was strong. She did what she had to do. She would keep on for as long as she could. Jordan eased onto the bed, lying on top of the blankets. He didn't want to sleep. He pulled her into his arms, and she snuggled closer to the warmth of his body. The cabin was warm enough, but fatigue made her skin rough and chilled.

The view from the bed out the window showed him that the sky was lightening up. His battery-powered radio was keeping him apprised of the latest weather reports. According to the reports, the snow was finished for now. The temperature wasn't expected to climb, so the accumulated snow wasn't going anywhere. He hoped the power would be restored before tonight, but he wasn't holding his breath. It was cold out, maybe not as cold as an Alaskan winter, but cold, nonetheless. He didn't envy the men who were responsible for repairing the broken electric lines or the men helping dig people out of their homes.

An hour later, he heard his cell phone ring. He swore softly and eased off the bed. He'd kept it charged, but now he wished he'd let the battery die. He didn't want anything to interrupt this strange interlude.

But it was probably his mother, and she would panic if he didn't answer. The phone number was his parents' house. "I'm fine."

"What a way to answer the phone," Lionel admonished.

"Sorry, I thought you were Mom." His grandfather was always welcome to call.

"How are you doing over there? Your mother said you found a woman on your way home the other day."

Jordan glanced at the woman in question. She didn't even shift position on the bed. "I did. My truck hit a patch of ice, and her car was in the way. Her car died on the side of the road, and mine is stuck in a ditch. Tomorrow I'll call a tow company and see if we have a chance of getting out."

Lionel heard an odd tone in his grandson's voice. "You don't sound upset. I don't know how happy I'd be if I were stuck with a strange woman. I love women, don't get me wrong, but they don't usually handle being cooped up very well. Your mother right now is getting restless, and she has a big house to occupy her."

"This woman has slept for two days. She passed out in the snow. She was running a nasty fever when I found her, and she was pretty sick. She seems fine now, but she's still worn out. Other than her taking up space in my bed, she's been good company."

"Does she want to be rescued?"

Jordan turned away from Samantha. "Probably. She'll want to get back to work. Frankly, she's not well enough, and being stranded is probably the best thing for her right now. I don't know how long she's been sick, but she can't keep her eyes open longer than an hour."

Lionel made a suspicious sound, almost like a smothered laugh. Jordan wondered what was so funny. "Pops, I don't know what you think is so funny, so why don't you just spit it out."

"You are. You want to keep her, don't you?" Lionel didn't stifle his mirth this time.

Jordan smiled into the phone but kept his own amusement to himself. "I don't mind having her around."

Lionel cleared his throat. "You know, when I met your grandmother, I knew she was the woman for me the day I met her because I could be around her for more than an hour and not be bored. She had a way about her that kept a man on his toes, no matter what the situation. Of course, I didn't know when I met her that I'd be marrying her, but I sure did like her company. Mostly I married her because she wouldn't let me so much as kiss her until I did. Your grandmother was strictly raised. Small town girl, through and through. I always hoped you'd find a woman like her. Your father went for a fancy woman, and it worked for him. I don't think it'll work for you."

"What are you getting at?" Jordan was well aware that his grandparents' marriage had been a successful one. It had only helped cement his conviction that marriage should be based on mutual goals, not mutual affection. The pair had worked hard at building his grandfather's business. But the affection was a nice bonus. His grandfather still grieved for the wife he'd loved and lost.

"I'm just saying that you sound awfully possessive about a woman you just met. If you want to keep her, then keep her. That's all I'm saying."

"That's all you'll say, too. You have a way of aggravating people with your half-formed advice. Just how do you suggest I do that?"

Lionel paused for a minute. "You know, times have changed. I think you're man enough to figure out how to get her to want to stay. Just take it slow and easy."

Jordan choked on a swallow of water from the glass he'd just poured. "Are you giving me advice on my love life? I hate to point this out to you, but I know what to do with a woman."

"Of course you do. I don't doubt it. But going about seducing the woman you want to keep is a little different from pleasing a woman you want to get rid of in the morning."

Jordan couldn't believe he was discussing sex with Samantha with his grandfather. "I think I can handle it."

Lionel let the subject go. "Are you wanting to be rescued tomorrow? I have my snowmobile. This woman's family must be worried sick about her."

"Not worried at all. She lives with her aunt and her little sister. I don't think her aunt cares where she is. She only cares that she's not at work. I think it might be best if I stayed far away from Sam's aunt."

"Sam? That her name?" Lionel interrupted.

"Her name is Samantha. Her last name is Brody. The only thing I really know about her is that she lives with her aunt and her sister and works as a waitress." Jordan broke off, then sighed resigned. "You can come fetch her tomorrow. She'll want to go home."

"All right, I will. Don't behave yourself, now. See you tomorrow."

"Right. Bye." Jordan punched the button to end the call. He turned around. Samantha was still asleep, just as he knew she would be.

Keep her, his grandfather said. It wasn't that easy. But nothing said he had to stay away from her. When his trip was up in Australia, if he was still interested in her, he could come back. Until then, he thought maybe he should think about keeping his hands to himself.

Keeping his hands to himself proved difficult. Every time he glanced over at her, flushed pink from sleep, he wanted to run his hands down the length of her body. Despite her thin frame, she had curves to her. The fact that he'd lain in bed with her, had felt her thighs around his hips, made staying away from her much harder than he'd anticipated. He could remember her taste, the feel of her body. He could remember the warmth of her breath and the heat of her mouth. But she was a virgin, and she might not fully understand what was happening between them.

By nightfall, which in actuality was only five o'clock, he lost his patience waiting for Samantha to wake. She'd gotten up at noon, only to fall back asleep by one. He told himself to keep his hands completely off her, but instead he found himself sitting beside her, rubbing her shoulder to awaken her.

"What?" Samantha rolled onto her back, trying to push back her snarled hair. When she felt a rough palm taking care of the task, she smiled and opened her eyes.

That smile threw all his good intentions out the window. How could a man resist a woman when she smiled at him like that? "You need to get up. You've been asleep all day. Are you hungry?"

She didn't feel hungry, but she thought she should

probably eat. "I suppose."

Jordan watched as she sat up unsteadily and flung the blankets back.

Samantha yawned and stretched her stiff muscles. "I take it the electricity is still off?"

Jordan didn't move. "It is. I expect it to be back on tomorrow. The snow out there might not be still accumulating, but it will take a while to move it. I'm afraid we're back to soup and bread."

"At least I'll be able to hold the cup. I feel like I've slept for days." Samantha swung her feet to the floor. Not an easy task because Jordan was still sitting on the bed, not moving out of her way.

"You should, because you did." He watched, amused, as she slid past him, her body brushing briefly against his as she headed to the bathroom. "I heated up some water so you can wash."

Samantha watched, amazed, as he set two buckets of water inside the bathroom. Jordan handed her a rag and some soap. "Thanks. This is just what I need."

Jordan chuckled to hide the sudden roughness of his voice. "I had one myself." He didn't add that he had made his a cold bath.

Half an hour later, Samantha came out. She had on another one of his shirts and the pants. Samantha was just grateful to have clean underwear. She left the bra with her uniform but pulled on the underwear he'd left with the change of clothes.

Her hair had been quite a feat, but having a tub to use, even without running water, had made the task easier.

"Sometimes I wonder if I shouldn't cut my hair short."

Jordan turned to see her come out of the bathroom. Her hair had been towel-dried, but the auburn mass looked almost black in the firelight. "Why don't you go sit by the fire? The heat will help dry your hair."

"I borrowed your comb." She had found it in the bathroom and didn't think he'd mind. She had used her finger to brush her teeth. She hadn't done that the night before, and her mouth had felt filthy.

"No problem. Help yourself to whatever you need." He wasn't worried about her germs. He wanted to get a lot closer to her and swap a lot of them. Jordan set the tray beside her and sifted a few strands of her hair between his fingers. "I like your hair as it is."

Samantha shivered at the touch of his fingers on her scalp. She had no idea how sensitive her body could be. She looked up at him, her desire plain in her eyes. She had no defense against him. Since he'd taken her in his arms that morning, she'd become painfully aware of him. She'd dreamed of him. Dreamed of his holding her, touching her, stroking her body with those calloused hands of his. She'd dreamed about things she hadn't known she was capable of imagining.

"Eat your soup. You need your strength." Jordan sat down beside her, knowing he was fighting a losing battle. Before the night was out, she would be his.

Samantha became aware of everything. Her heightened senses were disturbing but exhilarating at the same time. She became aware of the crackle of the fire. She could hear the wind blowing snow across the land and beating against the walls of the cabin. She was aware of the play of light and shadow on the wall.

Most of all, she was aware of Jordan. She was aware of every flex of muscle. She was aware of the pattern of his breathing, which became more uneven as the night passed. She was aware of the sound of his jeans rubbing together when he shifted position while he sat in front of the fire. She was aware of the fabric of his shirt, pulling and stretching over the muscles of his chest and back. She was aware of the way his nostrils flared when she came closer to sit near him, of the way his fists clenched on the floor across from her, as if he were fighting something within himself.

Jordan broke the intimate spell that had been weaving itself around the two of them when he spoke. "If you don't want me, Sam, you'd better go to bed."

Samantha hadn't expected the blunt statement. But with the way she'd been staring at him, she knew he'd reached the end of his control. It was frightening the way he was looking at her, as if he would devour her. There was something wild and untamed in his gaze, something she had never seen directed at her before. But in that moment, she couldn't deny him. Or herself. If there was a price to be paid later, she was willing to pay it. He would soon be gone and out of her life. And though she was scared, and though she knew she should say no, she didn't want to.

"I don't want to go to bed." Samantha held her breath and waited.

Jordan rose to his knees and walked on them to cover the short distance that separated them. He grabbed her waist and pulled her up from the floor to her knees, bringing their bodies together. "I told myself that we shouldn't do this. I don't care anymore."

The first touch of his lips on hers was a revelation. She could taste the leashed hunger in him. The feel of him, and the flavor of him, were indescribable. Never before had any man held her as if he were afraid she would be torn away. His hands were fisted almost painfully in her hair, but she reveled in it. The scrape of his tongue and teeth as they feasted on her mouth was more than she'd ever expected to feel.

"We'll eventually make it to the bed." Jordan set her slightly away. He reached past her, snatched the blanket from the bed, and laid it on the floor. He shifted Samantha until her back was on the blanket, her body bathed in the light of the fire.

Samantha watched as he unbuttoned his shirt. He didn't tear at the buttons but undid them slowly one by one, keeping his eyes on her, seeing if she was going to change her mind. He didn't have to worry about that. One small glimpse of his emerging chest and she knew she'd made the right decision. Her palms itched to feel that soft hair beneath her hands. She wanted to feel that mat of hair rubbing against the naked flesh of her breasts. She'd dreamed of that chest. Of having it, and him, cover her body once more.

Jordan pulled the shirt off the rest of the way. Samantha was staring at him, and it was with desire, not fear. "I hope you want me as badly as I want you."

"I do." Samantha whispered as she sat up to face him. He was pulling off his socks, something that turned her on more than she thought it should. She sat and waited, slightly disappointed when he left on his jeans.

"Your turn." Jordan grabbed a foot and brought her closer. He let his fingers drift up the legs of the loose pants, caressing her calves. His hands reached halfway up her thigh before the fabric bunched and stopped his progress. He used his nails to lightly scrape a path back towards her feet. He watched Samantha's head tip back and her hips arch to bring her legs more fully into his grasp. He stroked his palms back up her legs, then made a winding pattern down her inner thighs, brushing the backs of her knees. When she slid closer to him, he smiled and continued his journey back to her feet. When he reached the edge of her socks, he pulled them off, caressing her ankles and feet.

"Who knew legs were so sensitive?" Samantha held herself still, hoping to feel his hands on her legs again.

"Your whole body is sensitive, Sam. Your body is full of nerve endings. I plan on finding every one of them," Jordan vowed.

Samantha wasn't so sure she could survive it, but she was game. She went to the buttons of her own shirt, but Jordan's hands stopped her. "What?"

Jordan came over her, forcing her body back to the floor. "I want to do it."

But he didn't start with the shirt. His hands skimmed back up her legs, but this time the cloth kept her from feeling the texture of his hands. It didn't feel quite the same. When his hands worked their way up and brushed against the flesh between her legs, she was glad she was lying down. She didn't feel embarrassment; she felt only pleasure. But his hands didn't linger, and she tried to arch herself closer to him.

"Relax, baby." Jordan's voice sounded rough in her ear. He bit the edge of it, then smoothed the mark away. His fingers found the waistband of her pants, his pants, and started the descent. His hands circled her hips, his forearms marking the path his hands would follow. His entire body stroked hers as he made his way back to her feet, taking the cloth with him.

She closed her eyes, immersing herself in the feel of his body rubbing down hers. When the journey ended back at her feet, she heard him let out a pent-up breath. She opened her eyes to see him staring at her. Her shirt was bunched up at her waist, leaving her hips and legs exposed to his gaze. His shirt and her underwear were still covering her, but she felt as if she were naked. The fierce desire in his eyes was all she needed to see to know he liked what he saw. She couldn't bring herself to look at the fit of his jeans. She'd felt his arousal as he made his way down her body, but she just couldn't look.

Jordan saw the hesitation in her eyes and vowed to vanquish it. She was his, and nothing was going to stop him. He lifted her legs so that they were in the position needed for his body to slide easily between them. Instead, he let his hands roam the soft flesh of her calves and inner thighs. He let the back of his hands brush the soft cotton of her underwear, but he made no attempt to remove them. He bent his head, kissing her inner thigh. He heard the low mewling sound she made. It wouldn't take long before she was willing to accept him into her body.

But slow and easy was what his grandfather had suggested. He trusted the older man's judgment. Instead of pulling her underwear from her body, he eased himself into the cradle of her legs, adjusting her hips so that her body was intimately pressed against his. He knew from the way her eyes suddenly shot open that the feel of his jeans against the insides of her thighs aroused her but also frightened. "Just relax."

He'd said that before, but Samantha didn't know how she was supposed to do that when the long, hot length of him was throbbing and swollen against her body. She felt on fire, her body throbbing in tune with his. But he looked as if he were content to remain in his jeans, their bodies separated by the two layers of cloth. "Don't you want me?"

The question would have been ridiculous had a more experienced woman asked it. But Samantha wasn't, and she didn't understand why he was waiting. "I want you. Can't you feel it?"

She shuddered as he arched his body closer. "Then why don't you..." she broke off as he slid up her body then back down again, his body stroking the entire length of hers in one slick movement. She hadn't realized that a thin film of sweat covered both their bodies. She panted helplessly as he settled back more firmly between her legs.

"We're halfway there. I think I've found about half of those nerve endings I was telling you about." Jordan brought his mouth back to hers.

She was frantic for his kiss. She grabbed at him as she opened her mouth under his probing tongue, trying to lure him further inside. He didn't seem to need any further urging. The deep, wet kiss caused her body to pulse harder. She pulled her thighs higher up his body, arching herself as if she could break through the barrier of their clothes.

Jordan knew what she was trying to do, and he chuckled into her mouth. But he didn't move to relieve her of her underwear just yet. He instead brought his hands to her shirt and pulled it off the rest of the way in one quick movement. He bent his head, placing his lips between her breasts, savoring the clean smell of her body. The fragrance of her skin was intoxicating.

Samantha hadn't forgotten how sensitive her breasts were, but she hadn't known how badly she needed them touched and caressed. The wet tugging of his mouth, the steadily increasing pace and pressure, was almost more than she could bear. She could feel her lower body tightening with every hard suck of his mouth.

Jordan could feel what was happening to her, but he wanted to be inside her. He let go of her breast and calmly stroked the length of her body again. He felt her thighs go lax against his legs. He moved back to her mouth, craving another taste of her. She slid back from the edge, but her body was still craving him. He lingered at her mouth, then trailed a string of kisses against her neck. He copied the trail he'd made on her legs across her torso, skimming over her nipples and down over her belly. When he reached the edge of her underwear, he couldn't take it anymore. He shifted his body so that he could reach her. He didn't pull the fabric from her but wet it with his mouth.

"Jordan, please don't." All she could see was the top of his head, his blond hair lying against her trembling thighs.

"Not ready for that?" Jordan could feel the tension of her body, but it was not passion that was suddenly gripping her. Instead of showing her how much she'd like it, he climbed back up her body, making her sudden fear recede. He took his time, allowing her to be drawn back under his spell.

Samantha was hardly aware of his removing her underwear after he'd followed the line of her spine with his fingers. Like her legs, she hadn't known her back could be so sensitive. But he'd arched her closer, finding nerves with his fingers that she didn't know she had.

Jordan traced every inch of her body until he couldn't take anymore. He had to be inside her. He sat back and rose. He watched her eyes widen as he shucked off his jeans and underwear. He knew she was nervous. When she licked her suddenly dry lips, he knew she was also pleased with what she saw. Her body might not have been touched before, but it knew what it wanted. He'd aroused her enough that she wouldn't balk at the last second. Had she suddenly turned away from him, he would have died on the spot from frustration.

Samantha closed her eyes and wrapped her arms around his neck as he settled back between her thighs. The feel of him was different this time. Instead of his jeans, the hair on his legs teased her bare skin. There was no fabric to keep her from feeling the length of his arousal pressed against her. "Jordan, I want you."

"I know." He practically choked on his words; his need for her was so strong. He positioned her body better and began to slide into her, conscious of his much greater size. Her nails dug into his shoulders as he pushed inside a little more. "Am I hurting you?"

Samantha didn't hear him. She buried her face in his neck and held on. The feel of him stretching her body around his felt better than she'd ever imagined. When he pushed into her the rest of the way, she didn't feel anything but exquisite pleasure. Her flesh tightened around him, unconsciously using her muscles to bring both of them closer to the edge.

He groaned heavily, unable to hold himself still for even a second. She was hot and tight around him, and he couldn't hold back any longer. It didn't take more than a few short strokes of his body to push both of them over the edge. What amazed him was that he lasted that long.

Samantha clung and wept against his throat, unable to bear the huge bursts of pleasure that gripped her. Her body arched closer to his, bringing him as deeply into her body as he could go. The pleasure of feeling him moving inside her was more than she could bear. She wasn't sure what the sound she made was, but it was close to a panting scream.

Afterward, Jordan held himself still, staying inside her, feeling half dead from what they'd just shared. "Are you okay?" He'd heard her muffled scream, and he suddenly grinned into her hair, pleased with both himself and her. He knew she was more than okay.

Samantha's arms fell from his shoulders, her whole body suddenly limp. She didn't have the strength to move. "I think I'm dead."

Jordan crushed her deeper into the floor. He knew in a minute she would be unable to breathe. He somehow found the strength to roll over, bringing her with him, keeping his body firmly lodged inside her. "I think I'm numb."

Samantha snuggled closer to him, content with where she was. Eventually, though, her backside got cold. "We have to move. My butt is freezing."

Jordan squeezed the flesh she'd said was cold, and indeed it was chilly. "You'll have to sit up."

Samantha sighed and got up. She felt him slide out of her body, and it made her shiver all over. As good as it felt to have him inside her, it felt even better to have him move within her again.

Jordan watched her eyes dilate. He knew what she had just felt because he had felt it. "Later."

Samantha stayed silent, doubting that either of them would be able to move later. Twice more in the night, he proved her wrong. She reveled in it, unable to believe the pleasure he brought her. Finally, though, her body gave out, and she fell into an exhausted slumber.

Jordan, too, couldn't believe what he'd felt. But he wasn't going to analyze it. He knew that when he got back from Australia, he would be coming back for Samantha.

Chapter Six

Samantha knew reality would eventually intrude, but she hadn't expected it to come so soon. As she lay naked under a pile of blankets, she knew her time was up.

"Get dressed, honey. Fast." Jordan got out of bed and looked around for his pants. They were lying by the fireplace, a little too close to the fireplace. He picked them up and was surprised by the heat. The metal buttons burned his skin.

Samantha looked around for her clothes. They were tossed in every direction. She watched Jordan, magnificently naked, gathering them. He handed them to her as he took his turn looking his fill. "Why don't you take a nice hot shower? The electricity came back on early this morning."

Samantha blushed as she accepted the clothes. She wasn't accustomed to lying naked in bed or having a man stare at her body in open appreciation. She wasn't sure how she was supposed to act. But as her anxiety reached its peak, Jordan roughly brought her against him and thoroughly kissed her. She suddenly felt much better and much surer about what she had done last night.

"Go on." He released her as someone knocked on the door. "I don't want anyone seeing you naked but me."

Samantha obeyed. The water was nice and hot, and she let it pound on her sore muscles. Her body was stiff, probably a testament to having made love on a floor. Her body ached, probably a testament to having made love three times in one night. Samantha didn't consider herself naïve. She knew last night wasn't normal. But she hugged the memory of it to her. She couldn't regret losing her virginity to Jordan. Seeing as how she might never walk normally again because of him, she doubted she'd ever find enough regret in her to come close to feeling it.

When she turned off the taps and dried off, she heard voices. The new voice was male. She couldn't distinguish what they were saying, but the tone was friendly. It was probably someone coming to check on him. She had a sudden premonition that it was a family member. She didn't want to meet his family. But she couldn't hide in the bathroom like a coward.

When she finally left the bathroom, both men were seated at the small dining table. It held only two chairs. The other man looked a lot like Jordan, minus the gray hair. The man had a similar build and the same distinctive facial structure. She figured the man was his father. "Hello."

Both men turned in unison to look at her. Jordan's gaze held heated memories that caused her to blush. The other man's gaze held curiosity and a sudden wariness. He glanced over at Jordan, then back at her.

"Hi. You're a lot younger than I expected." He kept his gaze on her face.

She knew he could see her telltale blush. She tried to hide her embarrassment. "I'm twenty-two."

A grin split the man's face. "You look a heck of a lot younger. It's a pleasure to meet you, Sam. I'm Jordan's grandfather, Lionel."

"Grandfather?" Samantha tried to keep her amazement to herself, but she failed. "I thought you might be his father."

Lionel rose and held out a hand. "I had my son young. Have a seat."

"Oh, no, you sit." She tried to take a step back, but he had her hand firmly in his.

"Sit." Lionel tugged her into the chair. "I hear you've been sick. Coffee?"

She watched as he turned to pour her a cup of coffee, dousing it with cream and sugar without waiting for an answer. She could tell Jordan was hiding a grin behind his cup. She thanked Lionel and took a sip.

"We're going to go check out the vehicles. When we get back, I'll take you home, with or without the truck." Lionel zipped up his coat and waited.

She didn't want to go home. She wanted to stay. If she clearly deciphered the look Jordan was giving her, he didn't want her to leave either. But she had to work, and no matter what, she had responsibilities at home. "All right."

Lionel left the cabin. Jordan knew his grandfather would wait patiently on the small porch for him. "He called last night to say he'd be by. I knew you'd want to get back to work. Do you work tonight?"

Samantha nodded, blinking back tears. "I guess I'd better go. My aunt will be wondering what happened to me."

Jordan sincerely doubted it, but he kept his opinion to himself. "I'll call for a tow truck later for your car. Then I'll call my insurance company. I don't know how much damage I did to your car, but I hit it hard enough to bang my head on the steering wheel."

Jordan fished around in a drawer and pulled out a small notebook and pen. He held it out to her. "Here."

"The car wouldn't start before you hit it." Samantha frowned as he impatiently shoved the paper into her hand when she hadn't taken it from him.

"Write down your phone number. I'll give you my cell. What time do you get off work?"

Samantha made sure she wrote the numbers clearly. Her hands were trembling a little. "I don't have a cell phone, but my aunt and I have a landline. I get off at ten. The restaurant closes then. There's the cleanup, but that doesn't usually take too long. I should be done by ten-thirty."

He tore the sheet out and placed it in the drawer he'd left open. He wrote his cell phone number down and tore that sheet out. He folded it up and tucked it into her hand. He kept her hand in his and kissed her knuckles. "I'll pick you up. Can you get a ride to work?"

"I can call Kitty. I don't like to take my aunt's car, just in case something happens. Vivian can be a little hyper. Just last month, we had to take her to get stitches when she fell out of a tree."

Jordan pulled her closer. "I was like that. I drove my mother crazy. She said that for the first fifteen years of my life, she never got any sleep."

Samantha suddenly threw her arms around his neck and held tight. "I don't want to go."

Jordan calmed her by rubbing his hands in long sweeps up and down her back. "I know. I'll see you tonight after work."

"Okay." Samantha made herself let go. She'd never been the clinging type, and she didn't want to start now.

He placed a brief, hard kiss on her upturned lips and left her standing in the center of the room. As he pulled open the front door, he said, "We'll be back in half an hour, tops."

Jordan saw his grandfather waiting patiently. He had his hands in his pockets and was whistling. Jordan shut the door behind him. "I'm ready to go."

"She looks a lot younger than she said. For a minute there, I almost had a fit." Lionel didn't bother with preliminaries.

"I know. She's a year older than Amelia. Believe me, I'm grateful she's not eighteen. Or heaven forbid, younger. When you talk to her, you forget how young she is." Jordan hopped on the back of the snowmobile. His grandfather loved his toy. He bought it two winters ago, and he made constant use of it the minute there was snow.

It took only a minute to reach the two vehicles. Both were buried under two feet of snow. Lionel had brought a shovel. He handed it to Jordan. "You're a lot younger than I am."

Jordan cursed lightly, telling his grandfather what he thought of that. "You use that excuse every time you don't want to do something. You have an iron constitution, and shoveling snow wouldn't hurt you."

Lionel just watched. "I'll keep using it, too."

Jordan managed to get his truck uncovered first. With the wind blowing, most of it had drifted away from the vehicles. "Doesn't look like the plows came through but maybe once."

Lionel opened the door to the truck and found the windshield scraper. "You know how it is; these county roads never get plowed unless the other roads are done quickly."

"Could you do me a favor? Keep an eye out for a purse. Sam said she had it in her coat pocket, but it fell out. If the plows didn't sweep it away, it should be around here somewhere, though probably buried under a ton of snow."

"Where did you find her?" Lionel set the scraper down.

"Up the road a bit. I was just about to cut through the woods when I saw her." He started shoveling around Samantha's car. He watched Lionel wave at him as he headed up the road a bit.

When he came back, he was shaking his head. "There's too much damn snow out here. We can look for it later, once we get the cars uncovered. We'll try to get your truck out of the ditch first."

Jordan wanted to argue but knew Lionel was right. "I'll start it up."

Ten minutes later, and a lot of cussing later, the truck was on the road. His grandfather drove the truck back. Jordan had insisted that he warm up a bit. He knew how much his grandfather could handle, but he was a bit older than he looked.

Jordan followed behind on the snow mobile. They were both frozen when they stomped back inside. Samantha was at the stove. "What are you doing?"

Samantha set the pot she was stirring off to the side. "Heating soup. It's cold out, and I thought you might be hungry. It's not breakfast food, but it seemed like a better idea."

"I know I could use it. It's a long drive in the snow from here to my son's house." Lionel took a seat and a mouthful of the soup.

Jordan took the bowl she handed to him and set it down. But he didn't eat it. He took Samantha's hand and pulled her to the table. "You eat it. I'll get mine."

Samantha started to argue, but Jordan kissed her quiet. She blushed as Lionel stared at them, eyebrows raised. She bent her head to her soup and took a bite.

"He doesn't always have the best manners." Lionel kept an eye on Jordan while he said it. "You embarrassed the girl."

He pulled out a stool he kept in the small kitchen closet. "She'll get used to it."

Samantha didn't know how she felt being talked around, but she kept quiet. She wanted more time with Jordan than last night had given her. He seemed willing, if his last remark was any indication. She knew that he would be leaving for Australia soon. He'd probably go back to Alaska after that. He'd no doubt forget about her, except for maybe a few fond memories. Until then, she wanted to spend as much time with him as possible.

Samantha finished the soup and excused herself. She grabbed her uniform and the rest of her undergarments. She kept the pants on under the dress but put his shirt in the laundry. She couldn't help her blush as she pulled on her underwear. She hadn't worn them for long.

"I kept your pants." She pulled on her coat and waited

for the men to finish.

"You're more than welcome to them. You'll freeze as soon as we set foot out the door. I left your blanket on top of the dryer along with your sweater and your nylons."

Samantha had forgotten about them. She vaguely remembered wrapping the blanket around her waist to keep the cold off her legs. She grabbed her things and saw her boots were by the cabin door. She slipped her feet inside them. She shuddered as she remembered how cold she had been. She looked out the window. The snow looked pretty, blanketing everything, weighing down tree branches, and making everything look peaceful and undisturbed. But she could have died in that snow. For the first time since she'd been here, she realized how lucky she was that Jordan had found her. She had been too tired to deal with the ramifications before, but now she was awake and aware.

Jordan knew instinctively what she was thinking about. He wanted to go to her, but he didn't need an audience. Instead, he made enough racket to draw her attention away from the windows. "We should probably get going."

Samantha grabbed her scarf and wrapped it around her head. She felt cold, and she hadn't even left yet. Just the thought of trudging the distance to the truck made her shiver. She waited for the two men to put their coats and boots back on. She let them lead her outside, sitting between the two of them since her legs were the shortest and could handle sitting in the middle.

She quietly gave Jordan the directions. Other than that, she kept silent. She felt a deep sadness pervade her. She knew she would see him again, but that didn't help. She wanted to stay with him. When they reached her driveway, she stared out the windshield.

Jordan didn't let her say anything. He opened his door and helped her out of the truck. He led her to the front door. "I'll see you tonight at ten-thirty. Okay?"

"Okay." Samantha felt silly standing on her porch, not wanting to let him go. She stepped back from him. "Ten-thirty."

Jordan yanked her back to him. The kiss he gave her was intimate and had her blushing. He knew his grandfather was watching the display, but he didn't care. "Get your butt inside before I really embarrass you."

Samantha stumbled a bit but managed to get the door open and closed at record speed. Making love on her aunt's front porch would not only have shocked Lionel but also her aunt. She saw Rose standing near the hallway that led to her bedroom.

"I didn't know when to expect you back." Rose looked out the window and saw a bright red truck pulling out of her driveway. "Is that the man you were with?"

"Him and his grandfather." She hesitated to say who it was who rescued her. Rose knew, of course, who the Forrester's were. She might not be thrilled that it was one of them who'd rescued her. Being wealthy, and Rose being so poor, she resented the whole family, as did many of the locals.

"Roger has been calling here for you all day. He said you didn't call yesterday." Rose clicked off the television she had been watching earlier.

"I didn't work yesterday, so I didn't think I needed to call him." She pulled off her coat and toed off her boots.

"He wanted to know if you were coming in today. I didn't know what to tell him, so I told him you would be there."

Of course she did, Samantha thought; she certainly wouldn't tell him that she needed to take the day off. With this much snow on the ground, it wasn't as if the restaurant would be busy. Samantha supposed it didn't matter because she would have gone no matter what her aunt had told him. Right now, she just wanted a nap before she left for work.

"I'm going to call Kitty for a ride to work, then I'm going to take a nap." Samantha started heading for her bedroom. Then she stopped and faced her aunt. "Don't be surprised if I don't come home tonight."

Rose looked up at her niece in surprise. "Should I ask you why?"

Rose had never been much of a mother to her, so Samantha figured it would be senseless if she started to now. "No, you don't need to ask. The man I was with is going to pick me up tonight. I'll be over there."

Rose narrowed her eyes. "It's your affair, of course. But be warned, men don't always play fair."

Samantha thought about her father. The divorce allowed him to have his freedom back. Rose didn't want freedom; she didn't know what to do with it. For her, nothing had changed since the divorce. All she'd wanted from the union was a child of her own, and she'd used Samantha's father to get one. "Women don't always play fair, either."

Samantha left the room and went to bed. She stripped and fell naked into bed.

* * *

Samantha accepted the rib-cracking embrace with good cheer. "Kitty, I'm fine. I told you."

"Honey, you're going to give me nightmares. Thank goodness someone found you."

Samantha called Kitty earlier for a ride, and she had arrived right on time. Kitty was one of those people who would give you her lunch if you didn't have one, even if that meant she'd starve herself. Samantha knew her well. She also knew her tale of rescue would make Kitty's day. "You won't believe who found me."

"Tell me that your rescuer was male: tall, dark, and handsome. I need details." Kitty ushered Samantha out of her house and into the warmth of the car.

"He is tall. But he's blond, not dark haired. He does have brown eyes, but they're more amber." Samantha buckled her seat belt, drawing her story out.

"Is he someone I know?" Kitty didn't put the car in gear; she wanted details.

"It was Jordan Forrester." Samantha knew she had put it off long enough.

The high-pitched squeal sounded as if it had come from a much younger woman. "Are you serious? Jordan Forrester rescued you from the snowstorm?"

"He did. I told him I would tell you about it, but please don't tell anyone else. I don't want him to think I've been gossiping about him."

"Honey, you're the only one I gossip with. Well, my

husband too, but he just listens with half an ear. He won't repeat a thing."

"Thanks. But there will be gossip later. He's picking me up from work tonight."

Kitty was trying to concentrate on the road, but most of her attention was on Samantha. "Why? It was sweet of him to help you out, but why is he coming to pick you up? I'd take you home even if you weren't on the way."

Kitty was a mother figure, so Samantha had only given her an abbreviated version of the story. She'd told her Jordan came to her rescue, but she hadn't mentioned the fainting in the snow or the two days in bed. She didn't tell her about the night she'd spent making love with him either, because she didn't know how Kitty would take that. Kitty would probably be shocked. And the woman wasn't easily shocked.

Samantha fiddled with her coat pockets. "We got along really well while I was there. He wants to see me, but I have to work, so he's picking me up."

A slight humming sound was Kitty's answer. "I suppose spending three days together, alone in a cabin, might cause two people to become interested in each other. Just be careful, Samantha. He's not going to stay."

"I know. He's leaving in a week or so. Until then, I'd like to see him."

"Oh, dear." Kitty waited until they had arrived at the restaurant to say anything. "I know what that's like. But he's not the staying kind, like my Christopher. He'll hurt you and not mean to."

Samantha nodded, knowing what she said was true. It

was a little late for caution. She'd already slept with him, and she couldn't regret a second of it. He had made her feel so good. She had felt desirable. She'd felt special. It had been a long time since someone had given her that kind of attention, and she wasn't referring to the sex. He talked to her. He asked her things about her life. Going to bed with him was just the culmination. No, Samantha knew, she'd never regret it.

The shift was long and tiring. Samantha had napped before coming in, but she was still worn out. But it was Wednesday, and the restaurant wasn't as busy as a weekend. Samantha was silently dreading the rest of the week. She worked every day until Sunday. She hated the thought that what little time she had left to spend with Jordan was going to be interrupted by her very full work schedule. Maybe he'd be happy spending the late evenings or early mornings with her. She hoped so.

It was after nine when Jordan came through the door. It had been ages since he'd set foot inside Larry's. He'd eaten here often as a teenager. It drove his mother crazy that he took his money and bought greasy food with it. His mother was a health fanatic, and all their meals at home were a testament to that.

He saw Sam immediately. She was finishing up a table. She had seen him come in. At first, she had a shell-shocked look on her face. Then she'd given him an easy smile that made his blood rush straight to his jeans. He took a seat before he embarrassed himself.

"What are you doing here?" Samantha pulled out her notepad and tried to look busy. Roger was still a bit peeved at her for missing work. It wasn't her choice, but he had to complain.

"Getting dinner. I had enough soup and boiled eggs for a while. I didn't think you'd mind if I showed up early." He accepted the menu she handed him.

"I'm sure your soup at home would be better. But, no, I don't mind. You'll give Kitty a heart attack when she sees you sitting out here." Samantha knew she had other tables, but at the moment she didn't care.

"Told her?" He knew she would.

"I did. She thought it was great I'd been rescued by Jordan Forrester. Until I told her I'd be seeing you again. She worries about me."

Jordan thought maybe Kitty had the right of it. He was worried. He'd had all day to think about her and what had happened between them. He wanted to see her again when he got back from Australia. That hadn't changed. But when he thought about all the work he had to do and how much he wanted to go back to Alaska, he didn't know how things would work out between them. She deserved better than half a relationship with a man like him.

Right now, he was working past sudden guilt for taking her virginity. Okay, she was willing. But he had made her willing. He'd taken advantage of the situation. To make matters worse, he hadn't had any protection with him. He still didn't have any, and the drug store was closed. When it occurred to him that what he was planning tonight was missing an important ingredient, it was too late. Stores closed early in small towns, especially in the winter. He wasn't going to cancel his plans. If she got pregnant, he would deal with it. She would have to come with him, no matter what obligations she had to her family. She hadn't brought up the possibility. He decided he wasn't going to, either. She could be on the pill for all he knew. His sisters had been on it. He knew because nothing was kept secret in the Forrester household. Amelia needed hers. Lillian had taken them just in case.

Jordan hung around until closing and took himself outside to enjoy some cold, fresh air while the rest of the cleaning finished up. It took only twenty minutes before Samantha came out, Kitty by her side. He'd been expecting it. From the way Samantha talked about Kitty, he thought he was about to get the third degree.

"You could have waited inside." Samantha was wrapping her scarf around her neck as she headed his way.

"Didn't want to be in the way." Jordan watched in amazement as Kitty just waved at the couple. "She isn't coming over?"

Samantha waved back at Kitty. "I had another talk with her before we left. I didn't want her to embarrass you."

Jordan took her hand. "She wouldn't have embarrassed me. I know how women are. She worries about you, and she doesn't want you to be taken advantage of. I drove my sisters crazy any time they dared to bring a boy home."

"I'm an adult. I know what I'm doing."

Jordan pulled her to a halt and looked deeply into her eyes. "Are you sure? Do you really know what you're doing? It's been driving me crazy all day. My grandfather gave me a lecture about seducing young women. It was kind of funny because the night before he was all for my starting a relationship with you. He probably assumed you were older."

Sam heard what he wasn't saying. "And much more world weary. He didn't expect a young innocent in your bed."

Samantha didn't look angry. Jordan let out a relieved sigh. "Something along those lines. Come on; let's get out of here. I want you to myself until I have to take you home."

Samantha smiled crookedly. "I told my aunt I wouldn't be home tonight."

Jordan stared. "You didn't."

Samantha felt some of her assurance fade. "I just assumed you'd want me to stay with you. I didn't mean...I thought..."

Jordan halted her stumbling words with a rough kiss. "I want you to stay. I just didn't think you'd find the nerve to tell your aunt you were. I thought you would want to keep your involvement with me a secret."

"I'm not ashamed of what we did." She snuggled into Jordan's embrace. "I'm not going to take an ad out, though, if that has you worried."

Jordan ignored that. "We're going to freeze out here if we don't get in the truck."

"You ever done it in a car?" Samantha heard her words and blushed. "Sorry, I don't know why I asked."

Jordan pulled her to his side and opened the passenger door. "I think almost every single teenage boy has done it in a car, or at least come pretty darn close. It's hard to find privacy at that age. I had my share of encounters in my car. That was long ago, before I joined the Navy. Haven't done it in a car since before I graduated high school."

Samantha's cheeks were still pink. She was grateful that he hurriedly closed the door behind her. "Did you get the vehicles taken care of? What did the insurance company say?"

Jordan started the engine of his truck. "I did. Your car is being looked at. They're not entirely sure what it is yet. The engine is pretty old but should hold out. I'm not a car expert. I can change oil and check fluids, but cars were never my thing. My insurance will take care of the rest."

"I thought all men liked cars." Samantha settled into the seat and enjoyed the warm air blowing on her toes.

"I was into boats. I'm sure car and boat engines are similar. I just never tinkered with cars much."

"Is that why you joined the Navy? Because you liked boats?" Samantha remembered the cold depths of his eyes when she mentioned his job in the Navy. She didn't want to trigger bad memories.

"Yes. I thought the Navy would be perfect for me. I didn't want to be a stuffy businessman, wearing ugly suits and playing golf. I didn't care much about big business or making a fortune." Jordan watched the road, keeping his peripheral on Samantha.

"You must have done well with the Navy. You were in it for a long time. You must have gone far."

"I had what it took. You go through basic training like any other branch. I worked hard and made my way through the ranks. I realized quickly that my body could do the job. After a while, my mind was repulsed. I didn't know what else to do, but I realized I no longer had the right mentality.

I certainly didn't want to train a bunch of recruits who were still practically children. I came to hate it. I realized I didn't want to spend the next ten or twenty years taking orders. I finished my tour and left."

Samantha laid a hand over his. "I'm glad you left."

Jordan let go of the death grip he had on the wheel and clutched her hand. "Me, too."

The rest of the car ride was silent, and Jordan was grateful. His time in the Navy was a blessing; it had been during those years that he discovered what he really wanted to do with his life. At times, it was hard to remember when he'd been eager to be a naval officer. He alternately thanked his luck and cursed his fate. Those days were over now. He had other things to look forward to. One of those things he wanted was Samantha, if he could just figure out what to do with her and how to integrate her into his life.

He pulled into his freshly plowed driveway. "It took forever to get the snow out of here. My grandfather threatened to call my father if I couldn't handle it myself. Can't picture my dad out here with a shovel. He'd have paid someone a small fortune to come out here and do it for him."

It didn't sound like they had a good relationship, Jordan and his dad. "Would he come?"

"Yeah, he'd come if I asked. He'd have lectured me on family responsibility the entire time, but he'd have come." He saw Samantha's sad face in the light of the moon. "Don't worry about it. We get along fine after a few days. We're still at the 'welcome home, it's time for a nice lecture' stage of my visit. Once he settles down, things will be fine."

"My aunt doesn't lecture me. Maybe you should be grateful that he cares enough." Samantha said it matter-of-factly, but it left a small ache behind.

"Never thought of it that way." He didn't defend her aunt. It would have been a waste. "I guess I should be happy about it. It's hard to remember that when I want to pull my hair out and tell him to shut up."

Samantha laughed a little, if a little stiffly. She hurried inside the cabin, enjoying the lingering warmth from the banked fire. Jordan immediately headed to the fireplace and coaxed it into a nice, roaring fire. She felt her body begin to tremble as she watched him. He had the same effect on the banked fires inside her as he had on the real thing. She shed her coat and stripped off her boots.

"I have a present for you." Jordan rose from the floor, removing his coat and shoes.

"Why did you get me a present?" Samantha wasn't sure she was comfortable taking gifts from Jordan.

"You'll like this one, and it didn't cost me anything, but potential frostbite. Come here." Jordan held a hand out to her.

She took it without hesitation. When he told her to close her eyes, she obeyed.

"All right, open them." Jordan lifted the object he held with both hands.

Samantha opened her eyes. Then she stared in shock. "You found my purse."

Jordan was surprised by her lack of expression. Then she snatched it from his hands and threw herself at him. When her arms were firmly gripped around his neck, he grabbed the back of her thighs, pulling her legs high around his waist. He carried her over to the bed; his sudden need for her painful.

She lifted her weight higher up, not letting her grip on him loosen. The purse remained clutched in her fist. "You have no idea what this means to me. I've been just sick over the loss of that money. It might not sound like a lot to someone else, but it's a fortune to me. My aunt was so angry with me for losing it."

Jordan took the purse from her hands and tossed it across the room to land on the kitchen table. He managed to get his hands between their bodies, unfastening the buttons of her uniform. The old-fashioned-looking dress was bunched around her waist now as her legs tightened around him. The dress fell open, exposing a camisole and bra. "You are the most beautiful woman."

She doubted it, but he made her feel like she was. She leaned back in his arms, assured that he wouldn't drop her. He caressed her breasts through the layers of fabric. It felt wonderful. Her thighs tightened as her whole body responded to the firm stroking of his palms. Her nipples puckered and showed through the fabric, a sign of her heady arousal.

Jordan hiked her higher so his mouth could reach her breast. The position was a little awkward, but he managed. He backed her up against the wall beside the bed, his mouth feasting on her through the fabric. Samantha let go with one arm and pulled the straps off one shoulder. She switched hands and removed the other side. With her uniform and her undergarments now at her waist, Jordan took immediate possession of her bare flesh.

Samantha didn't know how long they had stood there, but her legs were trembling, and her body was on fire. "Jordan, I need you."

"I know, baby, I know." He didn't want to let go of her for a second. He thanked his lucky stars she had chosen not to wear nylons tonight. She'd be without a pair. He shifted her body again, bringing a hand between them.

Samantha gasped as she felt his fingers sliding between her legs, jerking her underwear to the side. "We can't do it this way, can we?"

Jordan unfastened his jeans. "Trust me."

Samantha did. She adjusted her legs around his waist when he lifted her slightly away from him. When she felt his naked flesh against her, she carefully lowered herself onto him with some assistance from Jordan. She heard his groan, but she was barely aware. She tipped her pelvis to deepen his penetration, letting her head and upper back rest against the wall.

Jordan managed to stay upright, guiding her hips into the rhythm he wanted. They were both panting, both quickly reaching the peak. He thrust into her as far as he could, one hand slapped on the wall beside her, and the other wrapped around her bottom.

Samantha felt her body tighten almost painfully, then release in a great rush of pleasure. She was hardly aware of Jordan's husky groan of satisfaction in her ear. She went limp in his arms, unable to do anything except let her head fall on his shoulder and let his hands support her legs still wrapped around his waist.

"I think I really am dead this time." Jordan let the wall support him as he supported Samantha. "Are you still alive?"

Samantha let out a satisfied sigh. "I don't think so. Can you make it to the bed?"

Jordan had his doubts. Somehow, he managed to get them onto the bed. When he had enough strength, he yanked off his clothing. He managed to get the bunched fabric of Samantha's dress and undergarments off her. She helped with the quilt, yanking it over their naked bodies.

"If this is the thanks I get for finding your purse, if you ever lose anything else, come directly to me." Jordan felt as if his muscles were made of water. He managed to bring Samantha closer, fitting her slight curves to the straight planes of his body.

Samantha giggled into his neck, her own body drowsy. "I will."

Jordan watched as she snuggled down and went to sleep. He didn't know how in the world he was going to be able to leave her.

Chapter Seven

Samantha fingered the postcard, feeling sad. It had been eight weeks now since she'd received it—two weeks after Jordan left. When she'd gotten the postcard, she'd cried a little, but the tears weren't sad then. Her heart had filled while reading the simple card, happy that Jordan was thinking of her.

But he had told her that things were a mess in Australia, and he didn't expect things to be wrapped up in three months. Then he said he had another job lined up after that. He told her that things would settle back down after the Fourth of July. That was four months away. He had told, not asked, her to wait for him. It was the first of March now. He said he'd be home to visit his family around the holiday, as was his custom. He'd see her then.

Staring at the card, she wondered if she would hear from him again. His three-month trip had become a six-month trip. She had no way of reaching him in Australia. She didn't even know if he was having his mail forwarded to him there. It had become important that she find him.

She tugged on a pair of fitted slacks and her nicest sweater. The time had come to make some decisions. The first thing she had to do was find Jordan. Then she needed to have a chat with her aunt. She wasn't looking forward to either plan. She hoped that Jordan's grandfather was around. She didn't want to have to explain herself to his parents. She guessed that they knew nothing about her.

"Are you going out?" Vivian skipped around the bedroom, still wearing her nightgown even though it was after eleven and she had been up since seven.

"Yes. I have to go out for a while. I'll be back later." She kissed the top of her sister's head and grabbed her purse. "Come on out of here."

Vivian obeyed, doing a little twirling dance as she went along. Samantha watched as her sister made her way into the kitchen where Rose was fixing an early lunch. "I'm going out for a little while. I'll be back later."

"Fine." Rose didn't face her niece. "Be back early. I'm going out later with Marie."

Marie was Rose's friend from Washington who was visiting family. The pair had been going out almost every night for a week now. Marie spent the day with her family, then hung out with Rose in the evenings at home when Samantha was at work.

"I will." Samantha grabbed her keys and headed out. Her car had been working great since Jordan had had it fixed. Jordan had left for Australia two weeks after they'd met. The day he'd left, he'd told her he had her car fixed. At first, she'd been angry with him. He'd told her he did it because he didn't want to worry about her. After the way they'd met, she could hardly blame him.

The drive to the Forrester family home was a short one. She assumed the family was there. As she stared up into the darkened windows, she knew she'd been wrong. She walked around the house to make sure, but there was no mistake. The house was closed up. The shutters were closed over the upper windows of the house, and there were dust covers on the furniture she could see through the windows. She knew the Forresters had several homes. It was silly to believe they didn't make use of them.

Defeated, Samantha got back in the car. She didn't know what she was going to do now. She looked up at the house. She could write to Lionel and hope that he would eventually get it. She had only this address for Jordan's family. With a plan in mind brewing, Samantha went back home.

She didn't know how Jordan was going to take the news that he was going to be a father. They'd spent two weeks together, and not once had either of them brought up using protection. For her part, she hadn't really thought about the consequences, even though her period had just ended a few days before she'd met Jordan. She wasn't naive, but she hadn't really thought she'd get pregnant, either. Tons of women spent months or more trying to conceive. Samantha didn't know if it was because she was young, or had been at the peak time for conception, or what. She didn't know if she was just more fertile than other women. Whatever the case was, she couldn't deny she was pregnant. Once she got over the shock of it, she found she was happy about it. Had she not wanted children, she would have been more concerned about birth control. With Jordan, she had unconsciously accepted the risk.

Samantha sat in her driveway when she got home. She hadn't told anyone. She could be eight or ten weeks, depending on which week in January it had happened. For two weeks she'd been with Jordan every day. When she wasn't working, they'd spent the day together, then made love during the night. It had been the loveliest of interludes. When she was working, he took her there and dropped her off. He would be there before closing, waiting for her. Afterwards, they would go back to his cabin. He had said he didn't want to share her with the world. Some of her clothes ended up there. A lot of her personal belongings somehow ended up there, too. She'd waited until he'd left before she went and fetched them. He'd told her to feel free to leave her stuff there, but she had told him she wouldn't feel right. She'd collected her things the day after he'd gone, locking the cabin up behind her.

Ten weeks. It was amazing how much could change in such a short time. Of course, it had taken considerably less time to fall in love. When Jordan left, she knew what she felt, knew why she'd allowed the intimacy between them to grow so quickly. She hadn't told him. She knew he wanted her. That wasn't something a man could fake. She didn't doubt that he cared about her. But he was not an easy man. In the short time they were together, he had been stubborn, testy, unruly, and obstinate. He had also been caring, tender, passionate, and incredibly inventive. There hadn't been one millimeter of her body he'd left untouched. Just thinking about what he had done to her with his hands and mouth, his whole body for that matter, was still just a little shocking.

She'd been innocent, but she'd thought she understood what happened between men and women. What she hadn't understood was how right it would feel with the right man. She hadn't understood how one person could hold your body and your heart on the line between exquisite pleasure and pain without going over. Jordan had never hurt her, not even that first time. Shocked her, yes; hurt her, no.

That was over now. Whether she would recapture those moments again remained to be seen. In the meantime, she had to do something. She wanted to tell Jordan about the baby first. He deserved to know before anyone else. Now she wasn't sure if she would be able to tell him before she had to tell those closest to her. She didn't know how to contact him. Lionel was her only hope in finding Jordan before he returned in July, assuming he returned as he claimed. It hurt her immeasurably to keep this from him, but she had to be realistic. He was far away from her. Six months was a long time to be away from someone you'd only spent two weeks with. He could have any number of women between now and when he returned. He might not want her at all once he was away from her.

She'd write Lionel a letter, asking him to contact her. If he didn't respond to the letter quickly, she'd have to tell Rose. It wasn't fair to keep it from her. She and Rose might not be the best of friends, but they were family. Rose had taken care of her since she was a young teenager. They might not be close, but Samantha had never gone without anything she needed.

Samantha trudged up the front steps of her house, her heart heavy. "I'm back."

Rose came out of her bedroom. "You're back early. If you don't mind, I'm going to leave early."

"I don't mind. Vivian and I will have a fine time." Samantha hung up her coat and watched Rose's retreating back. She loved Vivian. Rose was always sure not to take for granted that Samantha would be around to watch her sister. But Samantha had helped with her little sister since the day she'd been brought home. Vivian might not have a father, but she did have a devoted mother and a loving sister.

Afternoon drifted into evening. Vivian kept up a constant chatter about school and toys. Samantha kept checking the clock. Rose was an adult, but this thing with her friend Marie was starting to concern her. They were spending hours together. They'd been friends since childhood. Marie, too, was divorced, but she had no children. Marie couldn't have them. She sent gifts for Vivian all the time, playing honorary aunt. Though Samantha liked Marie, she feared what would happen if she and Rose spent a lot of time together. Rose was already dissatisfied with living and working here. Rose had started fantasizing about a new life in Washington with Marie long before Marie arrived.

Vivian was in bed by nine, and Samantha wrote a letter to Lionel. She sealed and stamped it, praying he'd get it soon and know how she could find Jordan. It seemed likely that someone in his family would know how to find Jordan in case of an emergency or a family crisis.

It was midnight when Rose finally came home. Samantha was dozing on the couch. She'd fallen asleep. She woke when the front door opened. "Is it late?"

Rose hesitated, then answered. "It's late. After twelve. What are you doing up?"

"I fell asleep on the couch. Did you have fun?"

Rose came into the living room and took a seat. "We

have to talk, Samantha."

Samantha sat up, pulling the blanket over her legs. "You're moving to Washington, aren't you?"

Rose looked guilty. "I am. I hate Colorado. I hate the cold winters and the excessive snow. I hate my job here. I only stayed because I married your father. Then it seemed easier to stay here and raise Vivian. You're an adult, and you can take care of yourself and make your own decisions. I think it's time I moved on. Vivian will settle into a new home. Marie is going to let me live with her until I can afford my own place."

"I know how you feel about Colorado. I don't feel the same, but I understand. When are you going?" Samantha wasn't surprised by her answer.

"I think it's best if I do this immediately. I won't sell the house until you have a place to live, but you'll have to make the mortgage payment." Rose was twisting her hands in her lap.

Samantha couldn't afford the house by herself, and they both knew it. "Put it up right away. I'll find something."

"Are you sure? I could really use the money from the sale."

Samantha thought of Jordan. If she could find him, he would help her. But Rose was right about one thing. She was an adult. She only stayed with Rose because Rose needed her financial help. If things got bad and she couldn't locate Jordan, Kitty would help her. "I'll be fine. I have a friend who will help me. If not, I have a job and there are cheap apartments in town. My car is in good shape, so things will work out."

"If you're sure?" Rose looked hopeful.

"I'm sure." Samantha rose from the couch. "We'll stay in touch. I'll want to know how you are and how Vivian is."

Rose stood. "I want you to know how much I appreciate what you did for me, Samantha. You didn't have to stay here and help these past four years. You could have left when you turned eighteen, had you wanted to, or any time in between."

"I could have. But you took care of me for a long time. Even now, you make my dinner, and you take care of the house. I think we have a fair trade."

Rose looked uncertain but suddenly looked resolved. "Are you okay? You've been acting strangely lately."

Samantha knew Rose was thinking about the two weeks she spent with Jordan. Since he'd left, she'd been a tad depressed. She tried not to let his absence get to her, but in the middle of the night, she'd reach for him, and when he wasn't there, it hurt. In such a short time, she'd gotten accustomed to having him by her side.

"I miss Jordan." Samantha thought about the baby and what that would mean now that she had to support herself on her own. "I need to tell you something. I wanted to talk to Jordan first, but I don't know when I'll see him. Since you're going to pack up immediately, it might be best if we talked about it now."

"What?" Rose looked suddenly wary.

"I made a decision. It was mine to make." Samantha knew her aunt would probably not be terribly surprised by her news.

"Are you moving in with Jordan?" Rose waited patiently

for a response.

"No. I'm having his baby." Samantha watched her aunt's eyes widen.

"I see. Did you do it on purpose?" Unspoken was how Rose had used Samantha's father.

"I didn't do anything to prevent it. He'll be back in July, so you don't have to worry about me. I'll be fine, and when he gets back, he'll help me."

Rose's words shocked both of them. "I can stay here until July."

Samantha's eyes filled with tears. It was unexpected and incredibly sweet of her to offer. "I didn't tell you so you'd feel guilty. I just wanted you to know. I can't tell you what it means to me that you'd stay, but you don't have to."

"Are you sure? I know we haven't been close, but you're my niece. I care about you."

Samantha gave her aunt a brief hug. "We'll tell Vivian tomorrow that she's going to be an aunt and about her big move to Washington."

"You are going to tell Jordan, aren't you?" Rose suddenly found her voice, her doubt about her niece's plans clear.

"I am." Just as soon as she could find him.

Vivian took the news with a squeal and shout. Moving sounded like a grand adventure to a five-year-old. Having a baby niece or nephew was just the icing on the cake. Rose had been taken slightly aback at her young daughter's easy acceptance of the move and the baby, but Samantha wasn't. Vivian would grow up to be an adventurer, Samantha was sure. The girl had a bright, spunky personality that would never be diminished if left alone. Samantha sincerely hoped nothing ever dampened her spirit.

All in all, the next three weeks were hectic. Kitty had been told about her aunt's impending move. She had been more than happy to extend an invitation to Samantha to stay with her until she found a place. Seeing how tired and queasy she'd been feeling, Samantha was more than ready to accept the invitation. She still hadn't told Kitty about the baby because she still wanted to tell Jordan first. But with three weeks of silence in response to her letter to Lionel, she knew she wouldn't be able to keep it a secret much longer.

By the fourth week, the house was empty and on the market. Samantha borrowed Kitty's empty attic to store her things. She'd begun looking earnestly for an apartment. She'd have all the contents of her bedroom to move, which didn't really amount to much. She had kept a small recliner, an end table, and a lamp from Rose. Rose had offered her money, which Samantha wasn't too proud to accept. The money would be used for the deposit on an apartment. They had shared all the expenses for so long that Samantha figured the money Rose had been saving was partially hers. And this way, when the house sold, Rose would keep all of the proceeds to put toward a new place.

She wrote Lionel again, this time telling him of her move. Jordan wouldn't know where to find her when he came back unless he came to her work. Roger was starting to get more and more difficult, and she wasn't sure how he'd take a stranger showing up at her work. Lionel now knew Kitty's address, and she had told him she'd write again when she found an apartment. There was still no response a month later.

"Honey, are you all right? You're looking pale." Kitty came and checked Samantha's forehead for a fever.

"I'm fine. I've been a little tired." Samantha was fixing dinner, enjoying the spaciousness of Kitty's kitchen compared to that of her aunt's old one.

"You haven't been the same since you got sick. It's been three months." Kitty couldn't keep the concern out of her voice.

Three months was right, and Samantha's pants were getting tight. She looked up at her friend. Her fiftieth birthday was tomorrow, and Samantha was going to disappear for the night. She'd already told Christopher. He'd been really sweet about her staying here, but he probably was looking forward to a night of total privacy. Samantha had a hotel room waiting for her.

Samantha put the lid back on the spaghetti sauce. She looked over at Kitty. There still was no word from Jordan or Lionel. She looked up at Kitty, her eyes solemn. It was harder to tell Kitty, who was more of a mother than a friend. "I'm three months pregnant."

The curse that erupted from Kitty surprised both women. "That bastard!"

"No. It's not like that. He doesn't know." Samantha took Kitty's hand, which had fisted.

"You didn't tell him?" Kitty's face was shocked.

"I don't know how to reach him. I've tried to find his grandfather, but I haven't gotten any response. Until then, I can't tell Jordan unless he contacts me first. It's not likely. He wrote to me shortly after he left and said he'd be back in July."

"You'll be what, six months by then?"

"About. I got pregnant in January sometime. I'd rather he know sooner, but I can't do anything about it." Samantha hoped he wouldn't make a liar out of her.

"Does your aunt know?"

Samantha nodded. "I had to tell her when she said she wanted to move. I couldn't tell her afterward; it didn't seem right. She offered to stay, but I told her I'd be fine."

"Got that right. You'll stay here."

"No. I should go. There's an apartment downtown. It just opened up. It's within walking distance of the restaurant. I think I'll take it. The owner said I could have a six-month lease. I have money for it."

"You think I'm going to let you move in by yourself? You're pregnant." Kitty took the spoon from Samantha, looking half-ready to smack her with it.

"Kitty, I appreciate everything, but you have a husband. If it were just you, it would be one thing. I can't force myself and a baby on both of you. Besides, Jordan said he'd be back. I have to trust that he will."

"Christopher wouldn't mind. We didn't have children, but that doesn't mean that we don't like them." Kitty tried to appeal to Samantha's practical side. "You're not going to be able to pay for a baby by yourself. You have to be prepared that Jordan won't be back."

It hurt to have Kitty say it. It hurt more to know that she could be right. Deep down, she didn't believe it. In her heart, she knew he'd be back. "I know."

"Honey, I'm sorry. I know you care about Jordan. He's the first man I've ever seen you act this way with. But he's not here, and nothing says he'll be back. He's not like you and me. He's a wealthy man. Most wealthy men don't have the same ideals as everyone else."

Samantha almost smiled at that. Kitty had a rigidly held belief that rich people were fundamentally different from everyone else. "Even if he doesn't want the baby, he will help me. Besides, he's not wealthy. He told me so himself. He said he wouldn't inherit his father's money because he doesn't work for the family company."

"He told you that? Believe me, that man has money. He spent a fortune on supplies for his cabin. Christopher kept quiet about the specifics, but the store was suddenly doing a heck of a lot better once Jordan started building."

"I know. He said that he sunk all his money into the cabin. I don't know if he has any more money than I do. But he has a good job, so I suppose he must be doing a lot better."

Kitty had her doubts, but she kept them to herself. "Just don't fool yourself into believing that he's Prince Charming. Okay?"

"Okay." Samantha took a seat and watched Kitty finish dinner. The apartment would look cold and lonely compared to the warmth of Kitty's kitchen. She knew that with or without Jordan, it was time she started taking care of herself.

The following Monday, she signed a lease and wrote another letter to Lionel.

* * *

Late summer in Australia was as beautiful as it was hot. Jordan sluiced more water over his head, hoping to cool off just a little. The difference between Alaska and Australia was getting to him. He thought he'd acclimate after a while, but the heat was so intense he didn't think he was going to. Those around him weren't faring any better. It was April now, so summer was winding down and the nights were getting cooler. January seemed a long time ago.

He had originally met up with a guide, but the man had taken off, taking a lot of Jordan's equipment with him, including his phone. He'd gotten out word that he was looking for the man, but down here he doubted the man would turn up. These men looked like they looked after their own. He'd hooked up with a small group of anthropologists instead. Some of them were students while others were professionals. The students looked ready to faint. The professionals looked right at home. The only one of the group who wasn't doing well at all was the biologist. The woman had whined and complained the entire trip. She was used to classrooms. It seemed this trip was her first expedition, and she wasn't happy.

Jordan used his shirt as a towel and then threw it aside. He heard a noise behind him. He grinned at the man who approached him. "How's it going?"

Lionel looked at his grandson, shaking his head. "When I asked to come here with you, I didn't even consider how hot it would be."

"It's summer." Jordan shrugged. His grandfather had asked to come along when he found out Jordan was going to be taking some pictures in the Australian Outback. It had been a spur-of-the-moment decision for his grandfather. They'd met up four weeks into the trip, shortly after his equipment had been stolen. His grandfather had always wanted to see the Outback. They both had gotten more than they bargained for.

"I've been places hotter than this. I just can't remember any at the moment." Lionel took a seat and stretched out. He was happy baking under the hot Australian sun.

"Maybe next time I'll choose winter instead of late summer. Alaska is sounding more and more like heaven." Jordan tossed a canteen of water at Lionel. The man was holding up well, but he was looking a little dehydrated.

"When are we reaching town? Your father is such a pain. He thinks I'm too old to be running around globetrotting. I hate to think what he's going to be doing when he's my age. He'll probably sit at home whining about how old he is."

"You know, Dad, he used to think anyone over fifty was ancient. He's that age now, and he's reassessing. Don't expect miracles, though."

Lionel chuckled. "He wants me to call and check in. I'm going to humor him only because I know he means well. Don't want him to have a heart attack or anything."

Jordan wanted access to a phone as well. He'd been here three months, and he was getting anxious. He had vowed not to call, but he wanted to talk to Sam. It alternately humbled him and ticked him off that a woman had this much control over him. The fact that Samantha didn't have to even try fried him sometimes. Then he'd remember her sweet responses to his slightest touch, and he knew he would call. He woke up in sweats that had nothing to do with the unrelenting heat. He ached so badly in the middle of the night he was sometimes tempted to take care of the problem himself. Instead, he laced his hands behind his head and gritted his teeth until he had himself under control.

"We'll get to town tomorrow. Probably in the early afternoon. Dad is probably in a panic by now." Jordan lay down, folding his hands behind his head.

"Yeah, he is. Your gal, too." Lionel copied Jordan's position.

"She doesn't expect me to call. I told her I wouldn't."

"But you admit she's your woman?" Lionel kept his eyes on the darkening sky.

Jordan swore. "Yes."

"I like her. You haven't said anything about her since we came; I wondered if it was just a fling after all."

"A fling? Pops, where did you get that word?"

"Your father. He calls Amelia's boys flings. He gets an exasperated tone when he says it, too. It's his fault she's the way she is. He never put his foot down with her. He was hard on you and Lillian, but Amelia came much later. She's as spoiled as they come."

Jordan agreed. "Sam's only a year older than she is, but she seems so much older. She understands responsibility. Amelia only understands money and the toys it buys."

"Your Sam might be after the same thing." Lionel played devil's advocate.

"I worried about it, too. But she didn't know I was Jordan Forrester at first. Then I told her I didn't have access to the Forrester fortune. She thinks I'm broke."

"That wasn't nice. I guess I can understand it, though. Your grandmother and I didn't have much money while I was building up my company, but she enjoyed the money once we had it. I worked hard for a lot of years, but I turned it over to your father long before it was time to retire. Your grandmother and I spent our last years together enjoying the fruits of my labor. Your father never learned to enjoy it. Then he got into politics and was never the same."

"I know. He can't understand why I keep away from the business. I make plenty of money, but it's not what he makes."

"Your Sam might be upset when she finds out you're not a pauper."

Jordan considered that. "You may be right. Either way, money or not, I'm going back for her."

"Going to marry her?" Lionel turned his head to look at his grandson.

"I don't think I have a choice." Jordan spoke the truth.

"You sound angry about it. I felt that way. I didn't want to get married. I wasn't sure I wanted kids. Then I met your grandmother. I didn't have a choice. There was no way I was going to let any man have her but me."

"I understand." He did. Now that he'd had Samantha, he wasn't going to let any other man so much as lay a finger on her.

The rest of the team came back, and the activity around the camp picked up. Everyone was moving slowly, not wanting to rush any more than they had to. It was just too hot. An hour later, everyone settled in to sleep. The thought of a hotel room and running water was enough of an incentive to go to sleep and get an early start.

By the next day, everyone was exhausted when they arrived at the hotel. The team was going to spend two nights here before moving on. Jordan debated whether he wanted to continue on with the team or find a different guide. He would do without a guide, but he had his grandfather to consider. He didn't want to risk getting lost or hurt while his grandfather was with him. Before he made any decisions, he wanted a shower hot enough to wash away the grime, then cold enough to give him a chill. The mediocre air conditioning in the room was a blessing, but the running water was a miracle.

He set the alarm by the bed after the shower to go off when it was time to call Samantha. Lionel had opted for the same. They were going to meet up later, after a good sleep. The whole team had checked in and had pretty much the same ideas. Bed sounded good, but a good meal and a cold beer later sounded better.

Jordan slept awhile but was awake before the alarm. He figured it couldn't hurt to call early. A minute later, he was worried. The phone company said the phone had been disconnected about a month ago. His mind raced with what that could mean. Logically, it was probably because she couldn't afford it. But the other reasons he thought of were not comforting. What if something had happened to her? When he met with Lionel an hour later, he was met with odd news. Samantha had written three letters to Lionel. The mail had been forwarded from their home to the house in Aspen where the family was staying.

"Did you have Dad read them?" Jordan couldn't drum up

interest in his food.

"I did. The first one asked me to contact her. The second said she moved in with someone named Kitty. The third said she was in an apartment. All three said that she wanted to get in touch with you but didn't know how. In the last letter, she gave her address but said she didn't have a phone in her new apartment. She figured if anyone knew where you were, it would be me."

"She had that right. Except you're with me." Jordan cursed. "She didn't say anything else?"

"No. They were short and polite. She probably just wanted to talk to you and let you know she had moved."

Jordan closed his eyes and rubbed his temples. "She moved two times. She mentioned that her aunt was thinking of leaving. The woman must have made her decision."

"She didn't say what she wanted. I wrote the address down." Lionel handed him a folded sheet of paper.

Jordan put it away without looking. It didn't matter where she was so long as he could locate her. He figured she wanted him to know she'd moved. If she were pregnant, surely she would have told Lionel. It had only been those two weeks, and she would have known long before now.

Jordan picked up his beer. He was glad she wasn't pregnant. He knew it was a possibility but probably a remote one. He knew enough about human reproduction to understand the risks. He hadn't had any condoms on him when they'd met. He could have rectified that, but by then he hadn't wanted to alarm her. And if he were honest, he liked not using them with her. The fact that he'd never taken that risk before with any other woman wasn't lost on him. Fact was, there had been a few different women over the years he'd felt some attachment to. He'd only felt a small fraction for them compared to what he felt for Samantha. When his grandfather asked him if he would marry her, he knew he'd thought about it before, but not all that seriously, not even when he thought about her getting pregnant. But once asked, he'd answered automatically and honestly. He would marry her when he returned and worry about children later.

He wanted them. It probably wouldn't be long before they had them. But he wanted this job, and the next one, out of the way before he discussed it with her. He'd marry her next year. This whole year was booked. He had a break coming in July, but after that, he had more work lined up. It would give both of them time to get used to the idea of marriage, and time to let his mother plan it. He knew his mother well enough to know she'd never speak to him again if he didn't allow her to plan his wedding, or at least help. So long as she kept it simple, he didn't mind going through the motions. He was sure Samantha would appreciate the gesture, and she was the prize he'd get in the end.

Decisions made, he finished his dinner. Maybe Samantha would join him on some of his jobs once they were engaged. He went to the hotel store and picked up some paper, an envelope, and stamps. He considered offering her the use of his cabin while he was in Australia instead of paying for an apartment, but decided she would reject his offer. He wouldn't be able to receive mail from her since he wasn't sure where he'd be; he told her to write back to Lionel and that he would get the letter through his parents.

Satisfied with his plans, he popped the letter into the nearest mailbox and went back to his hotel room to sleep. He needed just another month to finish this job, then he'd move on to his next one. He'd be in Australia another couple of months because he'd agreed to take some photos for another magazine. Jordan stripped and climbed into bed. Life was good.

Chapter Eight

July was going to be hot. The holiday had come and gone, and just a week into the month, everyone could tell it was going to stay hot. The sky was blue and few clouds marred its perfect blue surface. The weather people were saying this might be one of the hottest months in a long time. Few took the news in stride; the newscasters complained about the scorcher outside. Most residents of the state accepted it as part of the charm of Colorado. After a cold, snowy winter, a hot summer was a blessing.

Samantha was one of the few who cursed it. She was hot and tired, struggling to fit her bulk into her new uniform. Who knew that the human body could stretch like this? She was not yet even into her seventh month. She rubbed lotion on her burgeoning belly, trying her best to lessen the ever-forming stretch marks on her stomach. She finally buttoned up the dress, sitting down to rest. She looked at the clock. She had half an hour. It took only a few minutes from her apartment to get to work. She had stopped walking to work when the temperature hovered at one hundred degrees for its fifth consecutive day.

She looked around for her shoes. Her feet were swollen from long days on them, and she wasn't looking forward to putting them back on. She felt like she'd just taken them off. The doctor said it was normal. She was a small woman, and she was carrying an extra burden. Extra burden, my butt, Samantha thought. She was lugging a double load. When the doctor had told an already tense Samantha that there were two babies in there, she had almost fainted. One baby was enough. Two just wasn't possible. The extra bulk in her belly at six months told its own story.

Samantha didn't dare lie down. She let her shoes remain by the door until the last minute. She went to the bathroom, a trip she'd make a dozen more times before the afternoon was out, and went to the kitchen. On the fridge was the letter from Jordan, telling her he'd be home after the fourth. He didn't say which day. The butterflies in her stomach were going double time these days. Hiding her pregnancy for even a second was out of the question. She'd gained so much weight, mostly thanks to Kitty's cooking; she sometimes wondered if she'd ever get back to normal. At a little over five feet tall, it shouldn't be genetically possible for her to get pregnant with twins.

Oh boy, Samantha thought, as she felt the babies move. She tossed her empty glass of water into the sink and went back to the bathroom. Roger was getting fed up with her constant bathroom breaks. Kitty told him daily to shove it. She'd been very protective of her.

No one mentioned the fact that she wasn't married to her face, but she could see the question in everyone's eyes. No one asked her who the father was, but speculation was rampant. There was no shortage of gossipers. Everyone she knew, and some she didn't, had a suggestion as to who they thought it was. Since people had seen her with Jordan, he was the number one candidate. They were right, but she wasn't going to satisfy their curiosity.

For the rest of the day, Samantha thought about Jordan. She managed to not mess up the orders despite her distraction, but she was a bit slow. Most of her customers attributed it to her pregnancy. Fact was, other than the bathroom trips and being way too big for six months, she felt okay. Sometimes she felt so much excitement well up in her that she thought she might burst. Once her initial shock faded, she'd been happy about the baby. When the fear receded from the knowledge she was having two, she once again was thrilled. So long as the doctor didn't discover a third, Samantha was sure she could handle it. The doctor had laughed and assured her there were only two. Samantha was holding her to her word.

For the rest of the day, Samantha kept an eye out for Jordan. When it was closing time and he hadn't shown, she relaxed. For some reason, she expected him to show at the restaurant. She wasn't expecting him to show up at her apartment. Probably because she had gotten used to him picking her up from work. She climbed in her car and went home.

She was keeping her evening meals light. It helped her sleep when her stomach wasn't full. In the mornings, she was apt to make up for it. Once her morning sickness had faded, she had gotten her appetite back. She made sure she followed the doctor's orders, but sometimes her stomach won, and she'd gorge. She was eating her dinner when the doorbell rang.

Immediately, her stomach knotted. She unconsciously placed both hands over her babies. Taking a deep, steadying breath, she opened the front door. It was a toss-up who was more surprised, her or Lionel. Seeing the older man on her doorstep was a shock.

"What are you doing here?" It was her only greeting.

Lionel couldn't tear his eyes away from her belly. "Jordan asked me to come."

Samantha knew what he was staring at. She didn't think anything needed to be said. "Where is he?"

Lionel took her hand and closed the door behind him as he pushed his way inside. "I don't think we should talk about this outside. He's still in Australia. I came back on our scheduled flight. He had some trouble with his equipment, and he needed to straighten out some money issues. He asked me to come see you because he told you he'd be here. You never sent him your phone number, so he couldn't call. Why didn't you say something about the baby?"

His sudden anger surprised her. She wrapped her arms around her belly, suddenly on the defensive. "I don't have a phone. And I wanted to tell him to his face, not in a letter delivered through his parents. When I got that last letter in May, I figured another two months or so wouldn't hurt."

"Are you all right? You're not having any problems?" Lionel placed a hand on top of hers.

His concern made her eyes water. "I'm fine. Everything is normal. In about three to three and a half months, you'll be a great-grandfather."

"Jordan is going to be upset you didn't tell him." Lionel shifted his hand to her stomach. The baby kicked in response. "Active, isn't he?"

Samantha thought he had had enough of a shock. She

kept the fact that there were two to herself. "Very." She asked what she wanted to know most. "When is Jordan coming?"

"In a few days. He won't be far behind. His parents are having a fit, but that's nothing new. Don't worry. He'll be here soon enough."

Samantha felt the tears falling. She spoke softly between sniffles. "I want him here."

Lionel just chuckled and pulled her to him for a hug. "My wife cried all the time during her pregnancy. There was only one, but it was memorable. We were only blessed with one child during our years together."

"I don't mean to cry. I haven't really cried at all. I have just been edgy lately, knowing Jordan is coming, and knowing he is going to be shocked and probably upset."

"I'm going to tell him." Lionel tucked her head into his shoulder. "I promised to call him. He needs to know before he gets here. Let him get his anger out while he's away. It will be good for him to stew."

"I should be the one to call him." Samantha let her head rest where it was. At the moment, it didn't matter that he wasn't Jordan. She just needed a little support. "He should hear it from me."

"He doesn't want you to call. He's been edgy himself. He said he didn't want to be tortured by hearing your voice and not being able to do anything about it. He's as wild as an animal in a cage right now. It's best if I tell him."

Samantha was relieved. She would tell Jordan about there being two when she saw him. "All right."

Samantha and Lionel had dinner together.   Lionel

promised to have a long chat with Jordan and explain the situation to him. Samantha didn't ask for details. Once she closed the door on him, she fell into bed. She was physically and mentally exhausted.

Samantha spent the following weekend with Kitty, most of it inside. Samantha felt sticky and sweaty with her body being out of whack. The hot July air added to the existing problem. She was sitting outside again when another car pulled into the driveway. Christopher had invited everyone he knew over for an impromptu barbecue because he had bought himself a new grill, and he wanted to show it off. People had been arriving all day. Kitty was enjoying herself, alternately teasing her husband and entertaining their guests.

The sound of a familiar voice over the din of the party had Samantha sitting up. She shifted her bulky weight in the lounge chair and managed to sit up while maintaining her dignity. She saw Jordan's face over the crowd. He really was tall, she thought absently.

"Sam? Where are you?" Impatience dripped from his tongue.

"Jordan." It came out whispered, so she knew he didn't hear her. Still, he turned her way as she said his name. His eyes narrowed on her, as if he hadn't quite believed what his grandfather had told him.

Jordan felt a dozen different feelings flow through him at the sight of Samantha pregnant with his baby. When Lionel had told him, his first thought had been disbelief. Surely, she would have said something. She knew how to get in touch with him. Lionel had told him that she wanted to tell him herself. Though he understood the sentiment, he still felt cheated. Here she was, visibly pregnant, and he hadn't known until four days ago.

Then he saw her fear. Whatever else he might be feeling, he couldn't let her think he didn't want her. "Come here, Sam."

She heard the hoarseness in his voice. She had no choice but to obey. She quickly made her way to him. When she reached him, she gave a little cry and went directly into his arms. They closed around her in a viselike grip.

"I hadn't believed it." Jordan felt her belly against his, the life she carried moving slightly against him. He remembered another time she'd thrown herself at him in gratitude. He'd made love to her then. He wanted to now. Whispering voices around them reminded him that they weren't alone.

"I tried to find you when I found out, but I didn't know how to reach you. I had no idea Lionel had gone with you. I would have written to your parents." Samantha felt her tears wetting Jordan's neck, but she didn't care. The feel of him, the smell of him, was heaven. She'd craved this since the day he left.

"They might not have told you." He couldn't seem to let her go. He scooped her up into his arms; the added weight of her body was a shock.

She knew Kitty would forgive her for leaving so abruptly. With so many witnesses, someone was bound to tell her where she'd gone and whom she'd gone with. She let Jordan take her to his truck. The sight of the large red truck was a dazzling sight. "I thought you weren't going to be back for another week."

Jordan ignored her. He set her in the passenger seat. "We'll get your car later."

"It's at home. Kitty picked me up. She worries about me driving."

Jordan watched her, amazed at the size of her as she buckled her seat belt. He didn't have much experience with pregnant women, but to his eyes, she looked huge. Her body was slight, the bulk of her stomach looking more like a big medicine ball than a baby. She looked uncomfortable in the hot, high-backed seat. He turned the air on high, watching as she turned the vents her way.

"You should have told Lionel." He said it as he headed toward her apartment. He'd gone there first, but she wasn't home. She hadn't been at work either. Kitty had been his only other choice, and he was glad he'd been right.

Samantha felt guilt weighing on her. "I know. But you said you would be back after the fourth. When you didn't leave me a place to reach you, I figured it would be best if I just waited. I'd waited this long already. Your parents would have been the ones reading the letter to Lionel, and I just couldn't do it. I'm sorry if you're mad."

Jordan stopped at a red light and faced her. "I was mad. Not about the baby but mad that you didn't tell me. This complicates things. It would have been better if you had said something sooner."

"I know a baby is a big complication."

"You don't know the half of it. I thought you weren't pregnant because you hadn't said so. I had the first half of the year booked. I decided to work the rest of the year and put some money together. I planned on fixing up my place in Alaska. You can't live there with it the way it is now. I wouldn't ask you to. I was going to have you stay here in my cabin while I worked. I can't get out of the contracts."

Samantha sat in amazement. "When did you decide I would go to Alaska?"

He realized he'd been talking about plans she knew nothing about. "Never mind. The cabin can't be fixed before the baby comes. You'll have to remain in Colorado. You can't travel with me, either. Everything is a mess. I never would have signed those job contracts if I'd known you were pregnant."

If he wanted to make her cry, he couldn't have done a better job. She hadn't meant to harm his career or burden him further than she already was by waiting to tell him, but she had done just that. In retrospect, she should have made certain she wouldn't get pregnant in the first place. It was just as much her responsibility as his. Now not only had she made a mess of his career plans, she had to tell him she had gone and gotten pregnant with twins.

Jordan felt like a jerk. She was turned from him, but he could see the slight jerking of her shoulders, which told him she was holding back tears. She'd been so happy to see him. "I'm sorry, baby, I didn't mean to upset you. We'll work something out."

Samantha felt his hand rubbing her back. She turned her head to face him. "I didn't mean to mess things up. I know I should have told you. It was just hard, and I didn't want to tell your grandfather before I told you. He knew you'd be mad."

"I'm not mad. I'm upset. There's a difference. If I were mad, we wouldn't be having a calm, rational conversation." Jordan let out a pent-up breath. "We'll talk about this like adults. You didn't do this by yourself."

Samantha dried her eyes with the hem of her skirt. She tried for a small smile. "Okay. I have something else to tell you. It would be better if I told you now."

"It better wait until we get back to your apartment. I don't need any more shocks while I'm driving." Jordan saw she'd calmed down and felt better. When they reached her apartment, he carried her up the stairs. She protested that she could walk on her own, but he ignored her.

"Sit down. I'll get us something to drink." Jordan set her down on the only piece of furniture in the room. He grabbed the handle on the recliner, forcing her to put her feet up. He noticed she didn't even offer a token protest. He found the cups in the cabinets and some lemonade in the fridge. It made him smile when he saw his letter and postcard taped to the front of the fridge. She really had missed him.

"I hope lemonade is okay. Don't pregnant women get heartburn?" Jordan handed her the glass, and she immediately took a big drink.

"I don't have heartburn. I just have to go to the bathroom all the time." She took another large swallow. "It's too bad because I'm thirsty all the time."

"What did you want to tell me?" He looked at the end table and decided there was no way it would hold his weight. He sat on his haunches in front of her.

"Let me show you." She struggled with the handle and

managed to get the recliner down. She went to her bedroom. When she came out, she had an envelope in her hands.

He took the envelope from her. The wariness was back in her eyes. He opened the envelope and pulled out an odd picture. He swore loud and clear. "Is this for real?"

She flinched at his reaction. She took the sonogram from his hands. The picture clearly showed two babies. "I'm afraid so. This was taken recently. They're both boys."

It was more than he was ready to accept. He felt his own throat clench. He hadn't cried since he was a boy. He didn't intend to start now. "I can't believe this."

Samantha dropped to her knees before him, not an easy feat. He was sitting in the chair, holding the envelope. He had dropped into it as he'd realized what she was showing him. She removed it from his fingers, setting it and the envelope on the table. "I'm so sorry, Jordan."

He closed his eyes. "Oh, hell. Come here." He dragged her off her knees into his lap. "I've wanted to hold you for six months. Everything will work out. I'm upset. But it's not like you planned to keep it from me. We'll figure out what to do."

Samantha rested her cheek on his chest, loving the feel of his hands on her legs. He was rubbing her bare flesh in a light stroking motion. She shivered. It had been a long six and a half months. For her, it had been an exhausting six months. She closed her eyes, listening to the sound of his heart beating under her ear.

Jordan watched in amazement as Samantha fell asleep in his lap. He couldn't help but smile. He jostled her a bit as he got to his feet, but she didn't wake. She barely stirred as he stripped her and put her to bed. He tried not to look, but it was impossible. Besides her oversized stomach, her breasts were fuller, darker at the tips. Her skin was so pale he could see the veins in her breasts and chest. Her hips were rounder, her thighs a bit fuller. She'd been so slender before. Now her whole body was ripe, curvy. Her dark hair was longer. Her face was rounder. She looked softer than she had. Pregnancy agreed with her. It agreed with him.

He got into bed with her, leaving on his pants. If he took them off, there was no way he was going to keep himself from making love to her. She needed sleep. He needed his. He had left everything, dropped what he was doing, to come to her. When Lionel told him that she was pregnant, it was all he could do to not get on the first plane out. He had tried to calm down, but it hadn't worked. He did what he could and then made a reservation on the next flight. He would have to go back and collect his work and call the magazine to set up an appointment. For now, he just needed Samantha. The rest could wait.

* * *

It was the best dream she'd had in a long time. She felt warm and protected. As her eyes drifted open, she realized it wasn't a dream. Jordan was beside her, his body warm and strong, cradling her. His eyes were open, their amber depths staring into her. His blond hair was longer, the strands golden from their time spent under the Australian sun. His body looked harder; a few bruises and scratches marred his skin. She traced a finger over a particularly bad spot on his chest. She bent her head and kissed it, her tongue touching and soothing.

"Keep it up." He urged her mouth higher. In all the times he'd made love to her months before, she'd hardly touched him. She'd been shy. He understood. Now she was pregnant. The time for shyness was long gone. "Move your mouth farther up."

She knew what he wanted. She shifted so she had better access. His body was heating as her tongue made a light foray across his chest. His large hand guided her mouth to his nipple, encouraging her to sample the many textures of his body. She reveled in him, her mouth laving, her hands stroking. Her belly made it difficult to reach all the places she wanted from her position. She sat up and straddled his body as his hands urged her body back down to his.

His words were soft and encouraging. She missed him so much. She missed the way he held her. She missed his hands. She missed everything. She grabbed his hands, bringing them to her painfully swollen breasts. "Touch me. Lightly."

He did as she asked, aware that her flesh was tender. She returned the favor, her fingers drifting up his biceps, across the back of his arms. She traced the flesh across his shoulders and down his spine as he sat up, pressing her breasts against him. The first taste of her mouth was ambrosia. She tasted the same; her flavor made just for him. Her body made just for him.

"I missed you so much." Samantha grabbed for the waistband of his jeans, undoing the button and zipper as quickly as her trembling hands would allow. When she hesitated, he took her hand himself, bringing his erection into her palm.

She'd never touched him like this. She wasn't sure why she had the desire to now, or more pointedly, why she hadn't before. He had done these things to her; brought her pleasure she'd never imagined. She was sorry for what she had done by not telling him about the babies. He might not admit it, but she'd hurt him. She'd seen it in his eyes. She wanted to show him how much he meant to her. He seemed to want her to show him.

He guided her body and hands. He guided her mouth, showing her what he wanted. Her unskilled lovemaking drove him crazy. "I missed you, too."

Samantha smiled at him, her eyes misty. "I'm glad."

He kicked the rest of the way out of his pants, sorry now that he'd left them on. Though if he hadn't, she might not have taken the initiative to remove them. He fitted his mouth to hers, her tongue following his. He rubbed her whole body with his. He showed her how to do the same, taking her hands in his and moving her body where he wanted it. After a while, she no longer needed guidance. She knew what she wanted, knew what he desired. All the other times had been for her. This was for him.

She still straddled his lower body, but her bulk kept her from being able to finish what she started. "Jordan, help me."

He kept his hands gentle as he lifted her. When he brought her down onto his body, he kept his penetration slow and easy. It had been over six months. With her being pregnant, he was doubly careful. But Samantha eased the rest of the way onto him in one smooth movement of her hips and set the pace. She moved as quickly and as deeply as she could. She could feel every inch of him stroking in and out of her. She whimpered as she moved, unable to move as agilely as she once could.

He knew she was close to the edge. He knew he was. He lifted his hips, sliding deeper into her, knowing now that he wasn't hurting her. He moved his hands to where their bodies were joined, stroking her hot flesh. He felt her convulse around him at the first touch. He caught her under her arms and pumped himself one last time into her clinging heat.

Samantha was glad his strong arms were keeping her up because she felt like fragile glass. Her skin was so sensitized that she thought she'd shatter from the touch of him inside her. When his own release flowed into hers, she felt as if her whole world had righted itself.

Jordan eased out of her and settled her on her back beside him. He didn't ask her if he hurt her. From the rosy glow on her face, he knew he hadn't. "It's good to be home."

Samantha rolled and snuggled deep into his embrace, her body sated and her mind foggy. "I've been waiting so long."

"I know, baby." Jordan felt humbled by the absolute trust she had in him. No one, in all his life, had ever trusted him as she did. He didn't know what he'd done to have her in his life, but he wasn't ever going to let her go.

Her body was pressed against him, and as he lay there, he felt his children move. At first, he didn't know what it was. Samantha shifted onto her back as he slid his palms over her belly. "Do they always move like this?"

This was the first time he acknowledged the babies. She knew he accepted the reality of her pregnancy, but she wasn't sure the result of it had actually hit him. She put her hands over his, moving them to where she could feel what she thought were little hands and feet. "Right here. And here."

He straddled her body this time, letting his hands move freely across her stomach. "I missed this. I didn't even know."

"I'm sorry." She didn't know how many times she had said it, but she felt compelled to say it again.

He bent and kissed her quiet. "Don't be sorry. Things happen the way they happen. I shouldn't have left for so long. I should have brought you with me, to hell with your job or your aunt and sister."

"I would have wanted to go, but I would have stayed behind. You knew that. Had I known my aunt was going to decide to move as quickly as she did, I might have made a different decision. I wasn't sure you really wanted me with you. We'd only been together for those two weeks."

"I want you." Jordan moved off her and got out of bed. "I wanted you with me."

Samantha knew he'd never said that to another woman. The knowledge that he wanted her more than any woman before her was enough for now.

"Are you hungry?" Jordan yanked on his pants. "I'm starving. My body is still on Australian time."

"I am." Samantha rolled out of bed. She fished a nightgown out of her dresser. Jordan took the garment from her and put it on her himself. She felt her love for him swell to painful heights. She swallowed the words down, hugging him to her.

He felt his own heart swell, not analyzing what he was feeling. He was too busy plotting. One thing he had learned in the Navy was patience. And he knew how to plan. First, he had to tamp down his own impatience. Then he had to get her moved into his cabin. Next came marriage. When the babies were born, he'd move them all to Alaska. In between all that, he had to figure out how he was going to work and take care of Samantha at the same time.

He might be able to postpone some of the contracts. Some of them he might be able to get out of or turn over to someone else. In the meantime, he had to go back to Australia and finish up what he was working on. He'd worry about the rest of the contracts later. He was concerned about his professional reputation, but he was much more worried about Samantha. She was carrying twins, his sons, and she needed him.

He set her back from him but took her hand and led her to the kitchen. "Does your aunt know about the babies?"

"She knows about being pregnant. I haven't told anyone about there being two. I let your grandfather tell you about the pregnancy, but I wanted to tell you about the twins. I haven't even told Kitty, although she is surprised by my size. I think she already guessed it for herself. Or at least, it won't be a shock to her when I tell her."

"I'll have to bring you to meet my family. I think I'll wait until after the wedding. If I tell them before, I'll be harassed about making more formal arrangements."

Samantha stopped, her arm falling from Jordan. She looked directly into his eyes. "Do you want to get married? And don't tell me yes because of the babies. Do you want to marry me?"

Jordan knew women were sometimes overly sensitive. He figured he'd better tread carefully. Fortunately, he'd made the decision to marry her before he knew about the babies. With any other woman, it wouldn't have mattered how she felt. With Samantha, it mattered.

"Have a seat." He gestured to the stools she had at the counter. He helped her get her bulk onto the high stool.

She watched him as he rummaged through her refrigerator. She blushed as she realized he saw the letters she'd tacked to the freezer door. "There's plenty of food in there."

"I see." He was glad, too. Had she been struggling to feed herself these last few months, he wouldn't have forgiven himself. "We need to talk about marriage."

"Maybe." She wasn't going to agree wholeheartedly.

"I had planned on working all year. I don't deny that. I figured I'd see you in July. Then I figured I would see you between assignments. During that time, my mother would be having a field day planning a wedding. I never anticipated that you'd say no."

"You're very arrogant. You know that, don't you?" Samantha realized he had no doubts about her or her feelings about him. She doubted he used the word "love" in context with their relationship, but he was sure of her. It made her feel better about allowing him to marry her. She knew it was a typical reaction, but she didn't want to be married because she was pregnant.

"Call it what you want. If you don't want men to know how you feel, you should hold back your responses in bed." He slammed their meal onto the counter. He knew he was letting his temper get the better of him, but listening to her argue with him about marriage angered him.

Samantha bit her lip. She'd forgotten about his temper. "You're the only man for me," she said quietly. "I don't want to even try to hide what I feel. It's not that I don't want to marry you. I do. I just don't want you to do something you don't want to do because you feel responsible or guilty."

He came around to her side of the counter. He cupped her chin in his hand, forcing her to meet his heated gaze. "I don't feel guilty. You became my responsibility the night I pulled you out of the snow. Pregnancy has nothing to do with it. You might not have realized it then, but I did. You're mine. There is no guilt involved."

Samantha surrendered under the forcefulness of his kiss. Hadn't she felt as if she'd always known him? She'd had her first date at sixteen. In the six years that followed, no man had enticed her the way Jordan did. No man had made it past the kissing stage. He had stormed her defenses until she had none left.

Chapter Nine

"If I can manage it, we'll be wed before I leave." Jordan handed her a plate. He'd opted for omelets. His stomach was still a little queasy from traveling through so many time zones and a different hemisphere. Samantha probably couldn't handle anything too heavy but could use some protein. Omelets seemed like a good compromise.

"Okay." Samantha inhaled gratefully. Her stomach growled in response.

"Have you eaten today?" Jordan handed her a fork, watching her closely as she answered.

"I ate lots today. Kitty made sure I was fed. I'm just hungry again. You know the old cliché, eating for two. Well, I'm eating for three. The doctor likes to say that's just an old wives' tale, but I feel like it's true." She ate two bites, took a swallow of milk, and another two bites, all before Jordan had forked up one.

He kept his amusement to himself, figuring that laughing at her would just cause an unnecessary argument. "I'll talk to the local minister. I'll have him wed us."

"I'm not going to argue," Samantha said, forking up another bite.

"Good. I don't want you to. I have to go back for a few days, but I won't be gone long. We'll move your stuff tomorrow." Jordan took a bite, happy that he was feeling better than he had when he got off the plane.

She didn't work tomorrow or the next two days. She'd cut back her hours lately, so moving tomorrow wouldn't be a problem. She had figured Jordan would be back and she could work less. "The furniture can stay, unless you want it. I'll ask Kitty if she wants any of it. I just have my clothes and some personal belongings."

She was making everything a lot easier than he had anticipated. He hadn't known what to do with her bed and her living room furniture, not that there was much of it. He had thought she'd want to keep every piece. He had been prepared for an argument. His cabin just wouldn't hold all of her things. "We'll keep the dresser. The kids can use it."

Kids. Samantha swallowed her bite and set down her fork. "Are you happy about the babies?"

Jordan kept eating. He didn't want to make a big deal out of it. "I'm happy about the babies. I'm shocked about them, but happy. Eat your dinner. We can go watch television afterwards."

They did as he suggested. After cleaning up the mess from dinner, Jordan took her to the living room. He made her put her feet up in the recliner while he made do with the floor. It didn't take long before the day caught up with her, and Samantha was falling asleep. The nap earlier had not been enough.

"Come on, baby. Back to bed." Jordan simply lifted her off the chair and took her to bed. He left the nightgown on her, figuring she'd picked it to sleep in. He left her in bed, covering her up to her shoulders. The apartment was warm, but her skin felt cool.

Jordan left the bedroom door open a crack. He clicked

off the television and sat in the dark. He didn't prop his feet up. So many aspects of his grand plan were in the trash. Marriage would not take place next year. He'd have to call his friend in Alaska to get his plans going to expand and update the cabin, so that after the babies were born, he'd have a home to take his family to. His cabin here was small, though more modern than his other one. There wouldn't be room for four people once the kids got older.

Jordan closed his eyes and rocked slightly in the chair. He would need to set up at least one large crib, if not two. He'd have to see about getting clothes for the babies for the upcoming Alaskan winter. He wasn't concerned about the cold too much. Plenty of people raised children there and they survived just fine. Until then, he had to make sure everyone was comfortable here. The cabin might have a laundry area and a nice bathroom, but it didn't have separate bedrooms and living room. He couldn't have small children crawling around the living room and getting into the fireplace.

Jordan abruptly sat forward, dropping his hands between his knees. He took two deep, calming breaths. Sweet heaven, he was having twin sons. The woman in the bedroom had taken him by surprise. He'd just barely gotten used to the idea of getting married when he got sprung with this surprise. It hurt that she hadn't told him sooner. This type of emotional pain was not something he was accustomed to. His father might nag at him, grill him about his life, and complain that he didn't live up to the family name, but at no point had his father managed to hurt him. The fact that Samantha, a tiny female whom he hardly knew, had that power was disconcerting.

He'd been a loner most of his life, despite the family he kept in touch with. He didn't have many friends. Photography had appealed to him mostly because of its solitary nature. Like writers, he spent many hours alone. His Alaskan cabin was far away from a town or homestead. He had built this cabin here to get away from his family when they got to be too much for him to handle. Now here he was, soon to be a husband and the father of two.

Samantha stood in the doorway of her bedroom, watching Jordan. His head was bowed, and his hands were limp against his knees. He looked like a condemned man. She didn't want to force him into something he wasn't ready for. It wasn't noble of her or self-sacrificing. She'd grown up being an obligation, and she would not allow herself and her children to be nothing but an obligation to her husband.

"You don't have to stay. I can take care of myself." Samantha's words held a thread of steel, a strength neither of them had ever heard from her.

"It's overwhelming." He looked up, his eyes remote. She looked beautiful to him, with her dark auburn hair in loose waves around her shoulders. Her body still looked slender in the long nightgown. She had such small wrists and ankles he could so easily crush. With her delicate body were equally delicate emotions. He knew what she was thinking. If he were honest, she wasn't so far off the mark. He needed time to make adjustments, but he had run out.

"I suppose. You just learned about the pregnancy and now I hit you with twins. This situation isn't about fairness. It's about responsibility. I can take responsibility for my own actions."

"We're getting married." His words were absolute.

"Not if I say no." Samantha knew her bravado would falter at the least provocation.

Jordan rose to his feet. He crossed the distance between them in two long strides. "We're getting married."

Samantha started to shake her head, but Jordan took her face in his hands. She swallowed back her nervousness. He wouldn't harm her; she had no fear of that. But though she knew he'd never use his strength against her, his emotional weapons had the potential to be devastating. "I won't let you marry me because you feel you have to."

Jordan trailed his fingers down her cheeks and around the sides of her neck. He stroked the flesh there, enjoying the sudden racing of her pulse. "You come alive for me at the slightest touch. You melt around me so sweetly. Do you really think I'd let you go? I won't let some other man have you."

Samantha's body swayed towards him. "I don't want some other man. I told you. I want you." She slowly moved her arms up around his neck, letting him cradle the weight of her body. "I need you."

Jordan felt the words spoken against his lips. He needed her, too, and it scared him. Who would have thought that a small female could frighten Jordan Forrester? When he'd joined the Navy, he'd moved fast through the ranks. His commanding officers had told him he was made for it. And here this woman, with one touch, with one taste, could bring him to his knees.

Samantha felt the emotions move through Jordan. His

hands caressed one moment, then fisted the next. His body flowed against hers, then went rigid. She held him as he worked out whatever it was he needed to work out. She knew she'd thrown him a few curves, and he deserved time to come to terms with the changes that were going to take place. She'd had almost seven months to figure out what she wanted. She had more than accepted what would come. She had been getting anxious for her boys to come, all three of them.

Jordan backed her up to the bedroom and back to the bed. "You need to sleep. Stop worrying about the wedding. You don't have a choice."

Samantha considered arguing but figured it would be futile. Truthfully, she didn't want to argue, so her heart wouldn't be in it. Why argue when the man you loved was saying the things you wanted to hear? He might not have said he loved her, but she was content to let it be. He was with her, wanted her. It was enough.

He didn't try to make love to her again, although Samantha would have tried to find the energy. She curled up in his arms, now that he was beside her, and went to sleep.

Jordan kept her by him, knowing that no matter what the future held, she'd be waiting for him.

The next morning there wasn't time for worrying about the future. Jordan fetched some boxes from the store and brought them back to the apartment, all before breakfast. "I want you to take it easy. You can toss clothes in here, but don't try to move them."

Samantha smiled indulgently, promising not to overdo it.

"I'll let you move everything." In all honesty, she was surprised he didn't demand to do all the work himself.

"I'm going to call a friend of mine this morning. I was thinking about my cabin. It's really too far away from any towns. Instead of fixing it up, I'm going to buy a house closer to town. I'll have my friend start looking into it for me."

It had taken a minute to figure out which cabin he was talking about. "I thought you liked your cabin."

Jordan grabbed his shoes that he'd toed off when he came in earlier. "I got to thinking last night about it. I want to stay in Alaska. That hasn't changed. I realized the actual location doesn't matter. A house would be much better. We'll need the space. I can't bring my children to an isolated cabin in the middle of nowhere. If they got sick or something, we'd have to drive too far to get help. There are plenty of homes that aren't too far away from where I was living. We can keep the cabin for vacations or something."

The thought of going on vacation to an isolated cabin in the middle of nowhere held appeal. But it didn't have any appeal at all if they were going to live there. He was right. A house closer to civilization would be best. "You said we'd move after the babies come?"

"I don't want you to be uncomfortable." He grabbed his keys.

"They have hospitals there, don't they?"

"Of course they do. But twins come early. You're more than halfway there. Do you really want to move to Alaska now and risk having the babies in the middle of the move?"

Samantha shifted her body on the stool, knowing it was

futile to try to find a more comfortable position. "I want you to be happy. I don't care where I have the babies, so long as it's in a hospital. The state doesn't matter."

Jordan saw the truth of it in her eyes. He came over and placed a light kiss on her forehead. "You're sweet."

"Think about it. You're going to leave me to go to Australia in a day or two. You could look into homes in Alaska on your way back to me."

Jordan shook his head in amusement. "I hate to point this out, but Alaska is not on the way home from Australia to Colorado."

It suddenly occurred to her that maybe Jordan didn't have the money to buy a house. His cabin was rustic, and he did say he pumped most of his money into his cabin here. She didn't want him to worry about money. Money wasn't important enough to fight about. "Do what you think is best. I don't mind living in Alaska, and I don't mind having the babies there. But if you're more comfortable here, then that's what we'll do."

"You know, most females aren't so agreeable." Jordan unconsciously placed his hands on her belly.

Samantha batted her lashes at him. "I'm not just any female."

"That's the truth." He kissed her and let his hands rub her belly in circles. It soothed all four of them.

"Where are you going?" She murmured the words into his mouth, enjoying the slow, wet kiss.

"I'm going to go find my grandfather. I promised I'd see him. I'm going to have him help move your stuff. Go slow and pack what you can. Okay?"

"Okay."   Samantha released him reluctantly.   She watched in amusement as Jordan stiffly walked out of the apartment. His breathing was a lot faster than it had been before. He wasn't the only one affected.

An hour later, she had her clothes in boxes. Jordan and Lionel came through the door shortly after. "I finished the clothes. You can use the towels and things to wrap up the pictures that are hanging."

"Fine." Jordan looked around. "This won't take long."

Lionel started making turns around the room, pulling photos and pictures down. "Taking all these?"

Samantha bit her lip. Jordan's cabin here was quite small, considering. "Maybe I should just get rid of a lot of this stuff."

Jordan came over to her. As long as she didn't want to move her furniture, he didn't care what she took. He'd worry about unpacking her things later, after he found a house for them. "Take what you want. Leave what you don't. Don't worry about space. We'll make do until we move again."

Jordan let his grandfather tape the boxes up, and Jordan carried them downstairs to his truck. Lionel marked a box and set it aside. "When you get pregnant, you sure go all the way."

Samantha blushed a vivid red. "Yes, well, I didn't do it on purpose. I don't think twins even run in my family."

Lionel patted her hand. "What's one extra? Jordan will take good care of all three of you. It's going to be convincing the rest of the clan that he knows what he's doing that will take some time. They don't understand him or what he does for a living."

"You and he seem awfully close." Samantha wrapped a picture of her holding Vivian as a toddler and set it in the box.

"I understand him. My own son and I don't see eye to eye. Sometimes I wonder if he was switched at birth. He gets into politics and marries an eastern gal, not in that order. He had only one son and he wanted to make him in his image. Funny, because I never tried to do that to him. I never made Philip be like me. He was my only kid; I would have had more of an excuse. Lillian's just like her dad, and she married a man just like her father. I'm hoping that seeing you will finally get Philip off Jordan's back, once he calms down about the wedding and the babies."

The reminder that Jordan was a Forrester wasn't welcome. The more she thought about being a part of that family, the more panicked she got about meeting them. Lionel was a good man. She didn't doubt that Philip would be, too. But that didn't mean he'd approve of her. Then there was Jordan's mother, Ellen, and his sister, Lillian. Then there was Amelia. Amelia would never in a million years accept her as a member of the family. She'd hated her in high school. Surely she'd recognize Samantha from the restaurant.

Samantha stiffened her spine. Amelia would just have to get over it. The rest of the family would either accept her, or they wouldn't see the boys. That decision made, Samantha found renewed energy.

"Slow down, girl. If you hurt yourself, Jordan will have my head."

Jordan opened the door to the apartment at that moment. "What are you doing?"

Samantha turned her eyes, filled with determination, his way. "I'm packing. If you don't like it, tough."

Jordan raised his brows at that but let it go. She was moving a little faster than she should, but she'd tire out quickly enough. He wanted her happy, not swiping and spitting at him. Thinking of that reminded him of his cat. "McKinley is looking forward to coming home. I'm going to leave him with you if you don't mind."

Samantha had forgotten about the ugly orange tabby. "Where is he?"

"My sister has him. She's ready to have me come get him. I figured you could take him. You'll be in the cabin alone. He can keep you company."

Samantha wasn't sure a cat was company, but she'd take him. "I don't mind."

"Good. I'm leaving tomorrow."

Samantha bit back a protest. She'd known he wasn't staying. "I take it you're going to marry me when you get back?"

"Licenses take time. I'll be gone a week or so. When I get back, the paperwork will have gone through. We'll get married then. Afterwards I'll introduce you to the family. Like you said before, a little more time won't make a difference."

She'd said that in regard to waiting to tell him about the pregnancy. She was apparently completely forgiven. She cleared her throat. She didn't want to cry again. "I think everything's packed now."

The trio finished cleaning up. When they got to Jordan's cabin, he cleared out space for the boxes that wouldn't need to be reopened. "We'll unpack your clothes tonight. I don't want you messing with the boxes while I'm gone."

Samantha let that be. She helped fix dinner, and afterwards, Lionel took his leave. He left his phone number with her, as well as a new cell phone, telling her she'd better call should anything happen. She heard Jordan and him talking. While Jordan was away, she could expect plenty of visits from Lionel. It was sweet of both of them to worry about her. It wasn't necessary, but it would make Jordan feel better, so she wasn't going to protest. He'd already missed out on so much of her pregnancy, and he was entitled to worry.

Despite Jordan's command that she rest, she didn't sleep much that night. Jordan held her, then made love to her through the night. She understood his need. She didn't want him to leave her either. When she did sleep, she dreamed about plane crashes and Jordan falling off cliffs.

By dawn, she was exhausted and feeling weepy. She rolled back to Jordan, hugging his back.

"What is it?" Jordan felt tears on her lashes as she rubbed her cheek against his back.

She didn't tell him about her bad dreams. Instead, she hugged him tighter. "Nothing."

Jordan rolled in her arms to face her. She had dark circles under her eyes. He knew he should have let her sleep more, but time and again he'd reached for her. It had been a long six months. He probably shouldn't have tried to make up the time in one night. He glanced at the clock. "Promise me you'll sleep all day."

It wasn't a hard promise to make. "I'll sleep all day."

With her promise, he reached for her one last time. By the time he'd wrung one last cry from her, it was time to get up. He rolled from the bed and went directly to the shower. Samantha joined him a minute later.

"I'll wash your back." She pressed a kiss to his wet shoulder.

He handed her the rag. Half an hour later, he was dressed and ready to go. Samantha was wrapped up in his robe. "Lionel will be around, and he'll drop off the cat. Call him if anything happens. If I take longer than two weeks, I'll call you."

"Be careful." Samantha followed him to the front door of the cabin.

He pulled it open. "I will. Be good."

"I will." Samantha hugged him one last time. She wanted to tell him that she loved him, but she held back. It wasn't fair to hit him with it as he was walking out the door. When he got back and life settled, she'd tell him. Samantha went back to bed, using his pillow. She cried herself to sleep.

* * *

One week passed, then another. Jordan didn't call, which meant he'd be back soon. She kept the shiny new cell phone Lionel had bought for her nearby at all times. Samantha made a round of her tables, fetching drinks and pouring coffee. The restaurant was busy for a Thursday afternoon in July. The patrons were regulars, but they all apparently had the same idea. It was just too hot to cook at home. Samantha thought longingly of the bathtub at home. She wanted a cool soak.

"Take a break." Roger came around the corner, issued his order, and then left.

Samantha let out a relieved breath. Her feet hurt. Her back hurt. Her head hurt. Her stomach made life miserable in this heat, and with the cooking and baking, the restaurant was hot. The food today was making her sick. Thankfully Roger had decided he could relent and let her rest. She had decided to pick up a few more shifts. She wanted to put money away. Jordan had left her his bank card, but she hadn't used it much, except to buy a few groceries. She wanted to buy the babies' things when he returned. If he decided he could afford to house hunt, she'd wait. If not, there were a few things they had to buy.

Samantha sat and propped up her feet. She smiled at Kitty, who came around back. "Checking on me?"

"Roger's afraid you'll go into labor on duty." Kitty came around and rubbed Samantha's back. "He wants me to keep an eye on you."

"Roger certainly has proven he's not a complete jerk." Samantha leaned back into her hands, moaning a bit at the release of tense muscles. "That feels good."

"I know. Another three months or so to go. Twins come early, you know." Kitty kept up with the rubbing.

"So I've heard. I'm going to be unable to get out of bed soon. But Jordan will be back, and he can haul me up."

"He's due home any day now, isn't he?" Kitty knew

about their plans to move. "I'm happy for you, but I'm sure going to miss you."

Hormones were unpredictable things, Samantha mused, as she felt her eyes sting. All she seemed to be doing lately was sleeping and crying. "I'm going to miss you, too."

"Christopher and I have never been to Alaska. It will make for a nice vacation." Kitty squeezed her shoulder and let go.

"We'll still come visit Jordan's family, so I'll see you." Samantha wiped her eyes with her apron. "He visits almost every holiday. We'll visit you and his family."

"Talk to your aunt lately?" Kitty fixed Samantha a glass of iced tea, decaf.

"She's great. I've never heard her sound so happy. She's found a job, and Vivian is happy in school. In a few months, she's going to start looking for her own place. She wants me to visit and bring the babies. I told her Jordan will be busy working for a while, but that we'd come as soon as we could. I don't think he'll mind. Of course, it will have to be sometime next year, but that's not really that far away."

"Just think, with a photographer for a husband, you'll have tons of baby pictures to show off."

Samantha was startled for a second. "I hadn't thought of that. You're probably right. I'll have to email them to you and my aunt. Jordan's family, too, if they want them."

Kitty knew about her hesitations. "I know you're scared about meeting them. It'll be fine. People love grandkids, and you're giving them two. Lillian doesn't have any, so Jordan's will be the first."

"I'm just worried that they'll be so angry they won't

forgive him for marrying me. Lionel is great, but his father is another story. He gives Jordan a hard time. It doesn't seem to bother Jordan at all. He just does as he pleases."

"And it pleases him to marry you. Relax. They'll take it out on him, and it'll roll right off him." Kitty looked at the clock and winced. "We have another two hours to go. I'll take your tables. You just rest."

Samantha sat a few minutes longer then got to her feet. She had already eaten lunch, and it wasn't sitting so well. It would be awful if she suddenly rediscovered morning sickness at this stage. That stage had been mercifully brief. All in all, the pregnancy was going perfectly. Her doctor assured her the babies were healthy and growing as they should. All their parts and organs were visible on the ultrasounds. Other than being scared about giving birth, Samantha knew everything was fine.

She had an hour to go when she heard a commotion. She was in back, fixing up a tray. She turned to see Jordan storming through the doors.

"What in the world do you think you're doing?" Jordan's voice roared through the small space, causing everyone to turn his way.

"Jordan, you're back." Samantha didn't know what else to say. His eyes were snapping fire at her. His body was rigid, and he looked ready to go into battle.

Jordan grabbed her arm and dragged her out the back. "Have you lost your mind? What do you think you're doing?"

"You're hurting my arm." She tried to pull away, but his hand tightened. "Jordan, let go."

"If you weren't pregnant, lady, I'd toss you over my shoulder. You're lucky I don't take a paddle to your backside."

Samantha was immediately outraged. "Jordan, stop it."

He ignored her. He got her out of the restaurant, oblivious to the gossip suddenly erupting. He yanked open the truck door and practically tossed her inside. At the last second, he seemed to realize he couldn't throw her, so he boosted her up by the backside he'd threatened moments before. Samantha sat in a daze, torn between concern and anger.

Jordan slammed the door, then rounded the truck. He drove slowly in deference to her condition, but his hands were fisted around the steering wheel. The ride was done in silence. Samantha refused to speak to him. She rubbed her arm where he'd grabbed her, soothing the red mark left by his fingers.

They arrived at the cabin, and Samantha got herself out. The height of the truck forced her to use the door for balance. Samantha walked away in a huff. "Have fun walking back to get my car."

Jordan followed, his fury in no way abated. He slammed the cabin door behind him. "Are you trying to kill yourself? If you don't want to think about yourself, think about the babies."

"What are you talking about?" Samantha's vow of silence was forgotten.

"What did you think you were doing working? When I got here and you weren't home, I called Lionel. He said you've been working."

"Of course I've been working. What did you think I was doing?" Samantha placed her hands on her hips, the aggressive stance not intimidating with her protruding belly.

"I thought you had a brain. I thought you would have spent the last two weeks resting. Instead, I find you waiting tables for change. What is wrong with you?" Jordan's temper was slowly abating.

Samantha stared at him. She'd seen him angry before, but this was much worse. For the first time, she was a little frightened of him. She took a step away from him, coming up hard against the wall.

Jordan was oblivious. He had never been so scared. What was she thinking working? She was pregnant with twins. She had no business carrying heavy trays. They weren't destitute. He would take care of her. Did she think he wouldn't?

"Jordan, I don't know why you're so angry." She pressed back against the wall, her hands covering her stomach. The babies were suddenly restless, probably in response to their mother's sudden stress.

"You could have slipped and fell. You could have dropped hot food on yourself. You can barely walk." He rammed his hands through his hair, trying to get a grip on himself. He'd imagined all sorts of horrors, and he hadn't calmed down yet.

Samantha felt her knees trembling. "Jordan, I wasn't in any danger. Pregnant women work. It's not a big deal."

"My pregnant woman doesn't work. If you had an office job, maybe, just maybe, I'd have let you keep it for a while.

But you don't have one. You're not going back; do you hear me? I don't want to see or hear that you so much as set foot back in that place."

"I hear you," she whispered. He wasn't calming down as quickly as she'd hoped. She inched her way to the bathroom. She closed and locked the door behind her. She didn't want him to see her cry.

Jordan was suddenly disgusted with himself. What possessed him to pull her from the restaurant like an errant child? But it seemed to him that that was exactly what she was. He forgot sometimes how young she was. He dropped into the kitchen chair. He had gone after her like an animal, and he was sorry for it. His sudden, vicious temper was why he'd opted out of continuing his naval training after he'd passed some of the more vigorous training sessions. He didn't have the icy temper needed to get involved in the Special Forces units, as he was rumored to have joined. He'd contemplated it early in his career, but that desire had quickly faded. He had a hot, fiery temper. And he'd just unleashed it on the last person who deserved it.

But she had no business putting herself in danger. Visions of her falling on her stomach and bleeding to death had filled his brain. It was irrational; he knew that. It hadn't stopped him from storming into her work and publicly humiliating her.

He gave himself a minute; he got his emotions under control. He went to the bathroom door and knocked on it. "Sam, please come out."

There was silence inside the room. Then the door opened slowly. Samantha's tear-drenched face peeked at him. Her eyes were red from tears, as was her nose.

"Come out." Jordan held the door open in case she shut it again. Breaking down his own bathroom door would not have been a good way to end the fight.

She came out, not that she really had a choice. Jordan was a determined man. He got what he wanted because he worked hard at it.

Jordan pulled her with him to the couch. He sat back and pulled her astride his lap. "I'm not going to be a sweet, adoring type of husband. I don't have those things in me. When I'm mad, you're going to know it. I would never, ever hurt you, no matter how mad I get."

She leaned into him, her head resting on his shoulder. His arms came around her, rubbing her back. "I like this position."

He was forgiven, and he knew it. "You're not going back to work."

She sat up. There was no wariness in his eyes. No anxiety. He was very sure of himself. She sighed and laid her head back down. "All right. I didn't think you were going to go into a panic over it. I thought I'd put the money away. I cut back my hours, but with you gone, I thought it was a good idea to pick up a couple extra shifts. That way, we'll have extra money to put towards a house when you can afford it."

It came down to money. She thought he didn't have any, and it was his fault. When he'd met her, he hadn't trusted her to want him without money. Now she had worked herself ragged because she wanted to make sure they could afford to move. "Samantha, look at me."

She sat up again, placing her hands on his chest, enjoying the firm muscles under her palms. "I'm looking."

"I'm not poor. I have plenty of money. I could buy a house right now. It might not be a mansion, but it would be plenty big. I gave you the wrong impression. I don't have the Forrester fortune, but I have money of my own. When I said I put all my money into this cabin, it was the money I'd set aside from my Navy days. I have money from my photography, which isn't small change. I also have some money I inherited from my mother's side of the family put away."

Samantha saw the truth in his eyes. "You don't need the money I made? What about the birth and hospital bills? Babies aren't cheap, and I don't have insurance. I've already racked up quite a large doctor bill."

Jordan placed his hands over hers. "When it's all said and done, there might be some debt. It won't be anything I can't handle. Your future husband is going to be famous one day."

Of that she had no doubt. She let her hands lie still in his, but he pulled them down to her side, forcing her closer. She lay against him, listening to his quickening breath. She pressed her lips against his throat and placed a small kiss there. Samantha sighed contentedly. "Welcome home."

Chapter Ten

She'd rather have faced a firing squad than Jordan's family. He only gave her one day between the wedding and the day she was to meet his family. Samantha was sure the only reason Jordan gave her a whole day was that he wanted to recover from his wedding night by lounging in bed the following day. But the very next morning, he'd playfully slapped her rear and sent her to the shower. She'd glared at him, but he'd been oblivious. Now there was no way out of it. She might be fresh-smelling and looking her best, but she was still pregnant. It was definitely something she couldn't hide with all the makeup in the world.

Samantha braided her hair loosely and put on a minimal amount of makeup. She didn't want to wear too much or wear bright colors. She was wearing what she thought of as the obligatory sailor-style dress that most pregnant women seemed to own. Hers was not the most fashionable ever designed, but it fit over the bulk of her belly and covered her legs to her calves. Masking the size of her stomach wasn't easy to do. They had maternity pants at the store, but she was sure she'd be stretching their limits before much longer, so she'd opted for dresses. The fabric of her dress was already looking snug.

"You look pale. Are you feeling well?" Jordan helped her into her car, deciding to leave the truck at home. She hated having to be lifted into it, as he'd learned the day of their wedding. She'd been irritated with the truck and her unwieldy body. With her car, she would need a hand getting out, but Samantha said at least she could reach the ground.

"I'm fine. Just tired and pregnant. I'm glad you warned them and told them there were two grandchildren coming. I still remember the shock on Lionel's face." Samantha closed her eyes so he couldn't see how scared she was. They were going to hate her. She just knew it. She wasn't good enough for their son. He was the son of a rich businessman and politician, and she was the daughter of a truck driver. It might not bother her or Jordan, but it would probably bother his parents.

She was really nervous, and it surprised Jordan how much. She was hiding it, or trying to, but he was getting to know her moods fairly well. She hadn't tried talking him out of bringing her to his family's home, but you'd think he was taking her to meet his old naval commander instead of his family; she was that nervous.

He kept up a steady chatter as he drove, telling her about his family. "They'll all be there. My mother is furious with me, but she'll get over it. My father sounded more resigned. It was quite a switch. I think this is the last straw. Actually, it will be good for me. Maybe my dad will quit hounding me."

"Maybe he'll hound you more. Tell you that you should come to work for him because you have a family to support now."

Jordan was not appreciative. "Thanks," he said dryly.

"Just want you to be prepared for the worst. That way it

won't be so bad in actuality." Samantha could have bitten her lip for that blithe sounding statement. It was the truth, but she hadn't meant to speak about it.

"They're mad at me, not you. They'll love you."

As much as you? she wondered. He hadn't said the words to her. She hadn't said them either. She wanted to. Yesterday, after their wedding night, it had been bursting within her to say it. Something had held her back.

Samantha kept her gaze on the passing scenery. "How upset were they about the babies?"

"It's hard for them to be that upset when you're giving them something they want. My mother is angry I didn't tell her sooner. Frankly, I just didn't want her getting overly excited and finding you herself. I wasn't going to be around to protect you." He saw his little joke fell flat. "Come on, Sam. They're not ogres."

She shrugged. "I'm sure it will be fine."

Forget delicate sensibilities. Jordan had had enough. "Relax. You're meeting them. They'll love you. You're going to feel ridiculous later."

"Thanks a lot." She turned her back on him. She might have to be married to him, but that didn't mean she had to like it. She realized how crazy her thoughts were and realized he was right. She was being ridiculous. Hell would freeze over before she admitted it.

Jordan would have pulled at his hair had he thought it would do any good. He would have argued with her, too, but figured he'd just be wasting his breath. Samantha had gone stubborn on him. It was a new side to her he wasn't sure he'd seen before. As much as it irritated him, she was sexy when she pouted.

He always found her sexy. On their wedding night, she had seemed almost shy with him. He found her attractive, pregnant or not, but she was self-conscious. She kept covering herself and turning off the lights so he couldn't see her, never mind that they'd made love several times before the wedding. At one point during the night, he'd had enough. He'd turned on the overhead light and made love to her until she was begging. The memory was one he wouldn't forget.

She saw him looking at her, and she blushed. "Stop leering at me."

"Why?" He looked amused.

"Because we're seeing your family, and that's no way to be looking at me. They've had a big enough shock already." Samantha, whose back was still to him, turned when he laughed at her. "What's so funny?"

"Honey, you're adorable when you're mad. And leering at you won't shock them. My erection might, but my leering won't."

Samantha gasped and blushed. She stammered when she spoke. "I can't believe you just said that to me."

Jordan shrugged and pulled into his parents' driveway. "It's nothing but the truth."

Samantha managed to pull herself out of the car by herself. Apparently, Jordan needed to cool off. She couldn't work up any lusty thoughts when she was about to meet his family. The house looked like she remembered it. It didn't look sinister or anything. The cedar siding and roof made the house look rustic to fit into its surroundings. The size of it ruined the effect. Cabin, it was not.

She took Jordan's hand in hers as they made their way to the front door. "You know stress isn't good for the babies."

Jordan squeezed her hand in support. He opened the door and led her inside. He called out. "Hello."

A middle-aged woman greeted them. Jordan's mother had dark hair, several shades darker than his, and was perfectly styled and pinned. She was about average height. Her slacks were pressed, and her blouse was a pale shade of pink. She looked in dazed shock at Samantha. For a second, she wondered if Jordan had told her. Samantha numbly let Jordan lead her further into the house.

"Mom, this is Sam." He put his arm around her. She looked like she was going to bolt. "Samantha, this is Ellen, my mother."

"It's nice to meet you." Boy, that sounded trite, Samantha thought. The woman was still staring at her. She was released from having to say anything else to her when a man entered the hall. Though she knew this was Jordan's father, there wasn't much resemblance in the face. The two men were about the same height and had the same hair color, but they had very different features. Philip was much more classically handsome than his rough looking son. He was as well-dressed as his wife, a gold watch and wedding band visible.

Philip accepted the introduction but wasn't as silent as his wife. "For heaven's sake, Jordan, how old is she?"

Samantha paled. She hated looking juvenile. "I'm twenty-two. I'm older than I look."

Jordan's lips tightened, but he couldn't hold his tongue.

"Are we invited inside or not? Or are you going to interrogate us in the hallway?"

"Jordan, please." Samantha's voice was soft and pleading.

Jordan squeezed her shoulder. "She should be sitting and resting her feet."

Ellen found her manners. "Come in. We're just a little shocked, that's all. I never expected my son to bring home a pregnant wife."

Samantha heard traces of an east coast accent. She knew she'd come from somewhere east. Philip sounded like a native. She turned to look at Jordan. "Jordan worries." It was all she said in explanation.

"Got that right." Jordan took her to the living room. He spotted his grandfather, who was grinning like an idiot.

Samantha was giddy with relief at seeing a friendly face. "Hello, again."

Lionel rose and kissed her cheek. He took her arm from Jordan. "Don't let them bother you. They're sticks in the mud. Always have been."

"Dad, really." Philip helped his wife to a seat and sat beside her. Jordan was left standing by himself, watching his grandfather show his approval of his choice in brides.

"You can be trying at times," Lionel told his son. "It's where Jordan gets it from. You be nice now." He turned to Samantha. "How are you?"

Conversation drifted from topic to topic. Samantha's health, or more specifically the babies' health, was the first topic. They talked about the marriage, his parents admonishing them about the haste of it all. When the conversation went to where they would live, things became a little heated.

"You can't move your wife and two infants to Alaska. It's barbaric." Ellen spoke up for the first time since the conversation started. She'd let Philip question them.

"It's not the north pole. Relax. I'm not taking her to the cabin. I'm buying a house. A friend of mine is looking into it for me. I've decided to have the babies here so everyone can see them before we move. Samantha's agreeable either way."

"You can't want to move there." Ellen turned pleadingly to her new daughter-in-law.

Samantha felt a bit put on the spot. "If Jordan wants to live in Alaska, then we'll live in Alaska."

"You have a say. This isn't the Stone Age. My son is a bit old-fashioned, but he can't force you." Ellen rose. "I moved to Colorado for Philip, but I made him build this house and the one in Aspen. We also have homes in California and Florida. Alaska is too cold for babies."

Samantha didn't want to argue with her. But listening to the woman condemn her for following Jordan made her mad. "Jordan wouldn't put his children at risk. If you know him at all, you know that. Alaska is perfectly safe, and if Jordan wants to live there, then I'm okay with it. I don't need four houses. I just need one home and a loving husband. Everything else is just extra."

Lionel patted her hand in comfort. "It's all right, dear. She's just worried."

Jordan was watching Samantha. She wasn't sure what that look meant, but it made her shiver. She leaned back on the couch and let Lionel hold her hand.

The group was silent for a while. Samantha was almost grateful when Lillian arrived with her husband. Lillian was the consummate hostess and broke up the uncomfortable silence. She'd had plenty of practice dealing with awkward social affairs. Once the shock of seeing Samantha had passed, and knowing that she wasn't as young as she looked, things settled down. It took a while to find amusement in their mistake about her age. Eventually, she took it in stride.

"Are you feeling okay?" Jordan managed to get his wife back from Lionel. His grandfather looked like he was planning to keep her.

"I'm okay. Where's your other sister?" Samantha wrapped her arm around Jordan, using his body to rest against.

"She's being stubborn. She refuses to come downstairs. She's always been melodramatic. Apparently, my marriage is a personal affront."

Samantha was too tired to tense up, but it gave her something to think about besides his parents' sudden acceptance. His parents had calmed down and were being nice. Samantha hadn't expected any pleasantness from the visit. Lillian was apparently shockproof when it came to her brother. She chatted with Samantha like an old friend. Amelia was the only one who was going to be a problem. Thankfully, Jordan didn't seem to care what his youngest sister thought.

Samantha thought of telling Jordan that she knew his sister and not to worry about it, but figured it didn't matter. Amelia might recognize her from the restaurant, but she probably didn't remember her from school.

"What are you going to do once the babies are here? Do you work?" Ellen suddenly took an interest in Samantha.

For Samantha's part, she felt like she was being weighed and judged again. "I did work, but Jordan had me quit. He was worried. I don't know about after the babies come. They'll need me at home for a while. After that, I don't know. I'm just taking this one day at a time."

"Having twins must be scary." Lillian spoke up. "I think about having children, but I'm not so sure about the giving birth part. I'm still young enough. In a year or two, Martin and I will probably try for one."

"I wanted children. I helped raise my younger sister, so I know what to expect." Samantha looked down at the plate in front of her. She thought maybe it was chicken under all that sauce. The smell of it was making her sick.

"That's good, then. How old is your sister?" Ellen's eyes narrowed as Samantha stared at her plate like she'd been served liver.

"Five. She started kindergarten this year. She's my aunt's daughter, and they just moved to Washington this past March."

"Your aunt?" Philip spoke up.

Samantha explained that her aunt married her father to help raise her when her mother died. She didn't mind talking about her aunt. "She's happy in Washington."

"Why didn't you move, too?" Ellen asked, and Samantha could see she regretted asking when Jordan's eyes narrowed at her. "Never mind, dear, I think I know the answer to that."

Lunch progressed in a pleasant hum of conversation, but Samantha wasn't hungry. She couldn't bring herself to eat.

"Is something wrong with your lunch? We could fix you something else." Ellen smiled at Samantha, trying to be friendly.

"It's just fine. I don't feel well." Samantha gave her an apologetic smile. "I'm sure it tastes wonderful."

Jordan set his fork down. "You want to go home?"

She did, but she didn't want to be rude. His family was here to meet her, and it wouldn't be right if she took off at the first opportunity. Maybe it would be less rude on the second one. "I'm fine. I'm just not hungry."

"Are you sure?" Jordan was more than ready to leave.

"I'm sure." She tried for a reassuring smile.

After Samantha ate a few bites of the fresh bread set out, she started to feel a little better. She didn't think she could handle the chicken, but she ate a few of the steamed vegetables. Jordan must have seen that she'd had enough when, immediately after lunch, he made their excuses without asking her first.

"I remember the sick days. All three of my pregnancies went well, but there were days when just looking at food made me sick." Ellen followed the pair outside.

Samantha had bid everyone goodbye and gratefully went outside. Things had gone much better than she'd expected, but she wasn't ready to make it an all day visit. "I've been fine for the most part. It's just been this past week that I've had a hard time."

Jordan bid his family goodbye and kicked up the air in the car. Samantha wasn't looking well. "We could have left earlier."

"I didn't think it was polite to leave in the middle of lunch. I'm just feeling a little queasy. It's already passing." She turned the air vent on her, as she usually did, and leaned the seat back.

Jordan watched as she dozed off. A nap was the best thing for her, he knew. A visit with his family was stressful enough without adding awkward circumstances. Right now, he had a lot on his mind, and the silence was welcome. He remembered how she'd defended him to his mother. She knew him better than his family. She trusted him unconditionally. She said all she needed was a home and loving husband. He hadn't consciously equated what he was feeling with love. Love wasn't something he gave a whole lot of thought to. Mostly, it was an emotion that was useless to think about. It was either there, or it wasn't. It wasn't a gauge of his happiness. He loved his family. He would love his wife and children. That's what you did. It didn't need discussion or hours of contemplation.

He realized Samantha hadn't said she loved him, and women usually had to talk things to death. He supposed he took it for granted that she did. Some women might marry because they were pregnant, but Samantha wasn't one of those women. She was capable of taking care of herself. It made him happy. He didn't need a whiny, clinging woman who would question him every time he left the house. There would be times he'd be gone for long stretches, and he didn't need a lot of temper tantrums or ultimatums. With Samantha, he could enjoy her open affection because it wasn't stifling. With other women, the constant touching and hugging would have bothered him out of bed. With Samantha, it was as natural as breathing.

She loved him. He had no doubt. He loved her. He didn't think he needed to say it for her to know it.

When they arrived back home, he contemplated whether to carry her inside or wake her. He wanted to talk to her, but she looked exhausted. He knew she hadn't slept much in the past two days. Not that either of them was complaining about the lack of sleep. But right now, she needed rest more than a talk about their future.

He opened the door and lifted her out. She snuggled into his arms the way she always did. He set her on the couch instead of the bed. He grabbed the light blanket off the back of it and covered her up. She murmured to him as he pulled off her shoes, but other than that, she didn't move. He knew she'd be hungry when she woke, so he fixed her a sandwich and wrapped it up for later. In the last week, she'd gone through a whole large jar of peanut butter.

Jordan took a seat on the chair and read one of his photography magazines. He liked to read about the places other people had discovered and photographed. For now, it gave him a much-needed diversion. He'd had a lot on his mind lately, and the only time he had any relief was when he took Samantha to bed. It was easy to concentrate solely on her when he had her body wrapped around him. Sex with Samantha was definitely a major distraction.

When Samantha woke, she found a peanut butter sandwich shoved under her nose. When she finished it and a large glass of milk, she felt human again. "It's a good thing I like milk."

He smiled as he refilled her glass. "I want to talk to you about something."

"We're not going to fight, are we? I'm not feeling up to a fight right now." Samantha said it so calmly that Jordan stared at her. "What? We fight. Mostly it's your fault, but I'll take half the blame since we're married now."

He shook off the sudden shaft of desire that heated his blood as she stared at him so serenely. "I want to talk to you about what you're going to do when we move to Alaska. There won't be a lot to do, but you don't seem to need a lot of entertainment. You don't go out shopping or out to dinner. You do work, and that's been bothering me since my mother mentioned it."

"I'm not fond of waitressing. I'm sure I can find something else to do once the babies are old enough. Maybe I'll take up professional motherhood."

Jordan was getting diverted just by watching her drink a glass of milk and talk about being a mother. He really needed to get a grip. But the thought of getting Samantha pregnant again was definitely a turn on. "Stop interrupting."

He saw her eyes widen at the huskiness of his voice, but he persevered. "What I wanted to talk to you about was my photography. There's more to it than just taking pictures. There are the contracts to deal with, the cost of materials to add up, and supplies to buy. There's the equipment to keep in working condition. There is a lot of paperwork to deal with, and bills to pay. I thought maybe you'd want to help me. Run the office, so to speak. There will be times I'll be away for weeks at a time. Every time I return, I have a huge mess to straighten out."

"You want me to manage your career?"

"Something like that. You'll have your hands full for a time with the babies. We both will, though you'll have to feed them." He took it for granted that she'd nurse them. "I plan not to work while we set up the house, but I'll have to work eventually. By then, the boys will hopefully be sleeping through the night at least."

Samantha set her glass down. Knowing that he wanted to share his career with her made her happier than she imagined. She had envisioned him going about his career while she sat at home with the children. Since he was better suited to make the money, it seemed like the reasonable choice. She would eventually have found a job to keep herself occupied once the boys grew up, but this was even better. "I think that sounds great."

"With two children, it will be easier to have one of us at home at all times instead of trying to find reliable babysitters or daycare." He was relieved. When he'd thought she was made for him, he'd been thinking solely about sex. But she was made for him in every way. She understood his and her own needs. She didn't find it necessary to argue just for the sake of arguing. She wanted what he wanted, and it didn't require any persuasion on his part.

Samantha rubbed her stomach. "Do you think about having more children?"

"Of course." Jordan was finished talking about his job. Now he wanted Samantha.

"What do you mean, of course? You hadn't planned on

these two. I know you've taken it all in and dealt with it very well, but that doesn't mean you'll want more."

"You're my wife now. That means we will live together, grow old together, and raise our family together. I don't plan on anything but till death do us part. Even then, I have my doubts."

Samantha brushed her tears away. "Stupid hormones."

Jordan laughed. "I like them. They make you look feminine."

"I thought the big belly did that." Samantha let him draw her to the bed.

"That, too."   He kissed her quiet and diverted her attention.

* * *

Samantha was humming to herself as she set up the bassinets, swatting at McKinley who was taking a sudden interest in her. The cat had hid from her when Jordan was away unless he was hungry. Now all of a sudden, the cat wanted to play. The bassinets were apparently fascinating with their trailing ribbons and ties.

Jordan had decided the bassinets would be better to set up in the cabin instead of cribs. His friend Joel had found a house, and Jordan had flown up there to check it out. He had taken his camera with him, saying he would take plenty of pictures to show her. She had wanted to go, but she couldn't fly at almost eight and a half months. Jordan had not wanted to leave her, but she'd insisted. He'd left her just two weeks before to fill a contract he'd been unable to postpone. She didn't think this was any different. Just like before, she had his phone number. She had Joel's phone number. She had his parents' numbers, his sister's, and his grandfather's. Should she go into labor early, he would know within minutes. Like Jordan had told his mother, Alaska was not the North Pole.

None of that mattered now. She didn't feel like she was going into labor today, and he was coming home. He was due in about an hour. She wanted to set up the bassinets as a surprise. He'd gotten them from a consignment shop in town, but they had no linens. She'd gone with Kitty to get them. She picked up some little jumpers and some diapers. Kitty had bought her a slew of gifts. Even her aunt had sent her a package. Ellen and Lillian had taken her shopping yesterday for the rest of the essentials, so she was all set. The boys would be coming home in luxury.

Samantha finished fussing with the blankets. Though Jordan might not appreciate it, she'd bought matching curtains for the window closest to the bassinets. The teddy bear pattern might be a bit much for the cabin's rustic charm, but she liked them. The boys might never see the curtains, but it didn't matter. The corner of the cabin was now the nursery, and she'd gone all the way.

The knock on the front door surprised her. She wasn't expecting anyone. Kitty had already checked on her today, and Jordan's mother had called. With Jordan expected any minute, she doubted it was Lionel. When she pulled the front door open, she was filled with dismay.

"Hello, Amelia. I wasn't expecting you." Samantha reluctantly let the woman in. She had to remind herself that this was Jordan's sister, and she had to be polite, even if it galled her to do so.

"I see you know who I am." Amelia strolled into the cabin, her disgust plain on her face. "You'd think he'd do better for his mistress."

Samantha braced herself for an ugly confrontation. "I'm his wife, not his mistress."

"You weren't when you got pregnant. I'm surprised he even bothered to marry you. The brats are probably not even his."

"Do you have a reason for coming?" Samantha bit her tongue. She'd never wanted to hurl obscenities at someone before, but she did now.

"My point is that you should cut your losses. Jordan isn't going to stay with you. He's had tons of women. You're just one of many. He might fancy you at the moment, but it won't last."

"You didn't bother to meet me with the rest of the family. Why are you here causing trouble now? Is it because Jordan isn't here to defend me?"

Amelia sat and crossed her legs. Her arms rested along the back of the couch. "I felt it was my duty to warn you. You're not going to get any money out of him. He's hardly even a member of the family. He's more of a black sheep."

"This is all about you. You can't stand the thought that someone else might get a portion of what you think you deserve. You're a selfish brat, and you'll always be one. Get out of your brother's house."

"Make me." Amelia smiled maliciously. "You'll never see a dime."

Both women turned when the door opened. Jordan's smile faded. His amber gaze pinned his sister in place. "What are you doing here?"

Samantha answered for Amelia. She could already see the lies forming on the woman's red painted lips. "She's warning me I won't ever see any of the Forrester money. Also, the babies are probably not yours anyway, and I'm nothing more than a mistress, and you've had a lot of them. I think that about covers the scope of our conversation."

Jordan put his arm around Samantha. "Really? Then I guess I'll just have to give you my fortune, make sure I get you pregnant again just to be sure, and make love to you as often as possible. I can't have my mistress and wife left unsatisfied."

Amelia rose. "You can't possibly want her. She's nothing. She works as a waitress. She's a nobody. You can't mean to keep her."

Jordan released Samantha and grabbed his sister. He not-so-gently propelled her to the door. "The woman you're talking about is my wife. I suggest you learn respect."

Samantha watched as Jordan slammed and locked the door. He turned to her. Samantha's mouth opened, but nothing came out. She'd heard possessiveness in him before. Hearing him say she was his wife was not shocking. What had her gaping was the way he said it. There had been passion and desire in the simple statement. But there had been more.

"How long was she here?" Jordan yanked off his shoes and tossed them in the closet.

Samantha waited until he was standing upright before

she grabbed him. She was kissing him everywhere she could reach. As she rained kisses across his face and neck, she gripped his shoulders. "I love you so much."

Jordan chuckled into her mouth as he seized it with his. "I know, baby. I love you too."

"You do?" Samantha pulled back. He said it like he had said it a thousand times before.

He frowned at her. "Of course I do. I married you, didn't I? I don't marry women I don't love, even if they are pregnant."

"But you never said it." Samantha accused him.

"I did. Every time I've made love to you, I've told you. Your body was listening. Apparently, you weren't."

Samantha laughed and went back to kissing him. "Sorry. I'll listen next time."

"You're about to get a next time." Jordan wrapped her legs around him, not an easy feat with her belly in the way.

Samantha wrapped herself around him, body and mind. As he made love to her, she listened.

* * *

The shipping boxes were stacked around the room, but Samantha hardly noticed. She finished nursing Maxwell, but his brother Matthew had run out of patience. His fussing was getting louder. Jordan was rocking him in one of the chairs he'd bought, while she sat in the other. She'd teased him about the pair of rustic-looking rocking chairs, but he'd taken it with good grace. They fit in with the cabin's décor. From the photos of their new home, the five-bedroom ranch-style house was just as rustic.

"Ready to switch?" Jordan rose from the chair, eyes on Maxwell. "He looks ready to pop."

Samantha swapped babies. Nursing the two boys took a long time. It seemed like one of them was always hungry. She didn't mind at all. She nursed Matthew while Jordan burped Maxwell. The boys looked incredibly small in his hands. Maxwell's hair would be blond, like his father's. The pale wisps were only a few shades lighter. Matthew had dark hair, with a red hint to it. He would have her hair. Their eyes were still newborn blue, but she thought they might both have their father's amber eyes. They had his strong features; she could tell even now at only a month old.

"My parents will be here soon. My mother is still trying to talk me out of taking you to Alaska so soon. She's resigned to the move. Now she thinks she can try to postpone it."

Samantha switched sides and watched Matthew latch onto her other breast. She would miss Jordan's family. They had been kind to her since the boys had come. Amelia had even come to the hospital once. No apology had been forthcoming, but Samantha hadn't expected one.

"She got used to having you around. Your mother is still in shock that I carried the boys almost to full term. She's not alone." Samantha wiggled her toes and watched them, somewhat fascinated that she could see them again. The last month of pregnancy had not been easy. The last week had been the worst. She had hardly been able to move by then. Jordan hadn't minded. He'd just practiced his nonverbal communication skills until she'd thought she'd die from it.

In between practice sessions, he had practiced his verbal skills.

Samantha rubbed Matthew's back and watched Jordan again as he talked softly to Maxwell. "I love you."

Jordan smiled at her. "I love you, too." He knew she needed the words. He had found in the last few weeks that he needed to hear and say them, too.

The knock at the door broke the spell. Samantha settled back to enjoy her new family. She was loved. Everything else was just extra.

<u>From The Author</u>

I hope you enjoyed reading Loving Jordan. Though not the first story I ever wrote, it was the first one I felt was worthy of sharing with others. The journey to publishing this debut book has been a long one. Parts of me have always wondered if I ever would.

This title is part of the Contemporary "Retro" Romance Series.*

If you enjoyed the book and would like an email on my next release, please sign up for my newsletter @ elizabeth-castle.com/contact. Please be assured that your email will never be sold (I wouldn't want mine sold, so I wouldn't do that to someone else). You can also follow me on Facebook @ facebook.com/elizabethcastle.romanceauthor.

Also, if you enjoyed this book, or any of my other titles, please consider leaving a rating at your favorite retailer, Goodreads and/or Bookbub. And if you have the time, a text review would be lovely. Indie authors rely on readers like you to tell others how much you enjoy their books.

Happy reading,

Lizzy Castle

***About the "Retro" Series**: The books in the "Retro" series were written before I embarked on my romantic suspense publishing journey. I was devouring books from the 80s and 90s when I wrote them. I consider the books "throwbacks." I hadn't owned a cell phone for very long when I wrote these (2008 for those of you who are curious), which seems crazy.

Books by Elizabeth Castle

Single Titles:
    Going Home
    This Kind Of Love
    Chasing Hope
    The Babe & The Librarian (novella)

The Heart's Way Series:
    For Now and Always
    Ask Me To
    Say You Love Me
    Forever Love

Bennett Family Series:
    This Time Love
    A Bride For David
(novella)

All Of Me Series:
    All Of My Days
    All Of My Nights

Cantwell Series:
    Falling Slowly
    Unraveled
    Hidden Away
    Entangled

Contemporary "Retro" Romance Series:
    Loving Jordan

Visit elizabeth-castle.com for newsletter sign up and up-to-date releases.

www.ingramcontent.com/pod-product-compliance
Lightning Source LLC
Chambersburg PA
CBHW031043310726
48969CB00007B/2096